Some w...
about this D...

☆

"It must be good. I'm in it!!"
Daisy

☆

"There'll be no stopping her now (sigh)."
Daisy's mum

☆

"What the?!!!!! Who the???!!!!"
A surprised hippopotamus

☆

"Sorry, but I was busting."
An embarrassed rhino

Some words
about this Daisy book:

More Daisy adventures!

DAISY AND THE TROUBLE WITH LIFE

DAISY AND THE TROUBLE WITH ZOOS

DAISY AND THE TROUBLE WITH GIANTS

DAISY AND THE TROUBLE WITH KITTENS

DAISY AND THE TROUBLE WITH CHRISTMAS

DAISY AND THE TROUBLE WITH MAGGOTS

DAISY AND THE TROUBLE WITH COCONUTS

DAISY AND THE TROUBLE WITH BURGLARS

DAISY AND THE TROUBLE WITH SPORTS DAY

DAISY AND THE TROUBLE WITH PIGGY BANKS

DOUBLE
DAISY

RED FOX

UK | USA | Canada | Ireland | Australia
India | New Zealand | South Africa

Red Fox is part of the Penguin Random House group of companies
whose addresses can be found at global.penguinrandomhouse.com.

www.penguin.co.uk
www.puffin.co.uk
www.ladybird.co.uk

Penguin
Random House
UK

First published 2013

007

Set in VAG Rounded Light 15pt/23pt
Printed in Great Britain by Clays Ltd, Elcograf S.p.A.

A CIP catalogue record for this book is available from the British Library

ISBN: 978–1–782–95015–8

All correspondence to
Red Fox
Penguin Random House Children's
80 Strand, London WC2R 0RL

MIX
Paper from
responsible sources
FSC® C018179

Penguin Random House is committed to a
sustainable future for our business, our readers
and our planet. This book is made from Forest
Stewardship Council® certified paper.

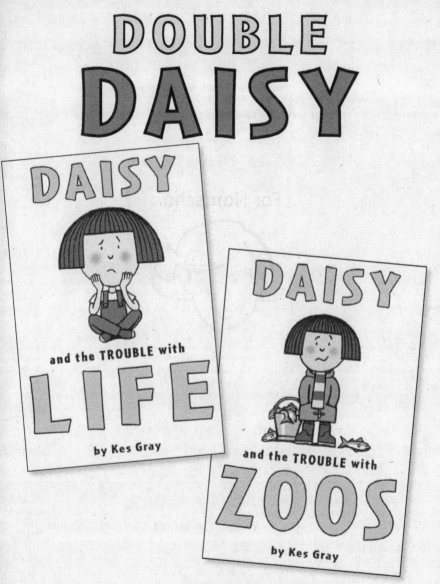

DOUBLE DAISY

DAISY

and the TROUBLE with

LIFE

by Kes Gray

DAISY

and the TROUBLE with

ZOOS

by Kes Gray

RED FOX

For Natascha

DAISY

and the TROUBLE with

LIFE

by Kes Gray

RED FOX

CHAPTER 1

The **trouble with life** is it's soooooo ooooooooooo not fair.

My mum says that sometimes life is like that, and that I should take this opportunity to think about things.

It's all right for her. She's not the one having to sit here trying to think about things to think about.

Thinking can be really hard when you're my age. Especially when you're grounded.

Excuse me a minute! . . . I need to go somewhere!!

CHAPTER 2

The **trouble with being grounded** is it's sooooooooooooo boring.

You absolutely can't go anywhere at all. There's absolutely nothing to do and absolutely no one to play with. Mum says I'm lucky that she's even allowed me downstairs into the lounge after what I've done. She says that most mums would have sent me to my room for about a hundred years after what I've done.

I bet Gabby's mum wouldn't. My best friend Gabby never gets grounded. Even when she drew on her lounge wallpaper with felt-tips, Gabby didn't get grounded.

That's the **trouble with mums**.

You can't swap them for other mums when you need to. Sorry – I need to go somewhere again! . . .

CHAPTER 3

I don't know why it's called "grounded" anyway. If you ask me, if someone says you're grounded, then it should mean you have to stay on the ground. No hopping and jumping, flying or parachuting. That's what grounded should mean: staying on the ground. Whether it's inside ground or out-side ground, it shouldn't make any difference. As long as you're on the ground you should be OK.

Both my trainers were on the ground in the hallway this morning when Gabby called for me. Gabby is my secret sister. We're in a secret club – in fact it's so secret, only me and her are in it. Every Saturday we take it in turns to be club leader and think of things to do. Last week it was my turn to choose, so we dug a mud trap in my back garden. Then we magicked Tiptoes, the cat from next door, into a lion and tried to get him to fall into our trap. But he wouldn't. He just stayed on Mrs Pike's wall and refused to come down. That's the **trouble with cats**.

They only ever want to do cat things, not lion things.

In the end we had to bang him down with a spade. Gabby hit the wall with the spade handle and I kicked the wall with my trainers. Tiptoes jumped down then all right. He jumped down off the wall on the very first bang. Only not into my garden, into Mrs Pike's. He never comes into our garden any more. In fact I didn't see him on the wall for five days after that.

Gabby says he must have seen us making the mud trap, and it would have been better if we'd magicked him into a hippopotamus. Hippopotamuses love mud.

Gabby's definitely right, so that's what we were going to try today. A better spell and a bigger trap. Except we can't now, because I'm not allowed out to play. Thanks to Mum.

Excuse me a minute. I need to go somewhere again! . . .

CHAPTER 4

When Gabby called for me this morning, I was dressed and ready and everything. I saw her walking up the path from the lounge window.

She'd brought her own spade to help dig the trap with, a stick for stirring the mud and hopefully some words that rhymed with "hippopotamus". That's the **trouble with writing magic spells**. There are hardly any words that rhyme with "hippopotamus".

I promised my mum I would stay grounded on the ground in the back garden with Gabby. I promised I wouldn't lift my feet up off the grass or anything, apart from when I needed to put my foot on the spade, but she said, "Stop right there . . . Sorry, Gabby. Not today, Gabby. Daisy's grounded. Daisy did something extreeeeemely naughty yesterday and she'll be staying indoors today. I'm sorry to spoil your fun, but it's important that Daisy does some long hard thinking today. She needs to think long and hard about the naughty thing that she did yesterday. And most importantly she needs to learn her lesson."

How poo is that! Uh-oh! I need to go somewhere again . . . !

CHAPTER 5

The **trouble with long hard thinking**

or even **short hard thinking** is it makes your eyebrows ache.

Especially if you've spent all week trying to think of words that rhyme with "hippopotamus".

Whippo-plop-a-bus, zippy-what-a-fuss, kipper-platypus, drippo-spottiness . . . I've tried absolutely everything. But none of them work.

That's the **trouble with magic spells**: if they don't rhyme properly the magic doesn't work properly either.

Anyway, I've given up thinking about hippopotamuses now. What's the point of having a magic spell that rhymes really well with hippopotamus if you can't use it?

I'm NOT allowed out to play with Gabby today, so we CAN'T dig a bigger mud trap and we CAN'T turn Tiptoes into a hippopotamus. Thanks to MUM, Gabby and me can't do any secret club things AT ALL today. So THAT'S THAT!

My mum says if I keep frowning and the wind changes, my face will stay that way. Well, she should have thought of that before she grounded me. It's totally her fault I can't go out to play with Gabby and it's totally her fault I'm having to frown so much.

I mean, just think. If it had been windy this morning when I opened the front door, my face might have turned into the worst frowning face in the world.

For ever!

And who would have been to blame?

It wouldn't have been me.

It wouldn't have been Gabby.

It would have been Mum! It would have been totally all Mum's fault.

And our front door's.

OOH dear . . . I need to go some-where again. Back in a minute!

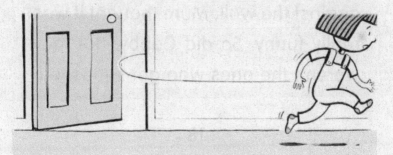

CHAPTER 6

The **trouble with our front door** is it sticks.

You have to pull it really hard to open it. I pulled it really hard when Gabby called for me this morning. I pulled it so hard I nearly squashed myself against the wall. Mum thought it was really funny. So did Gabby. But they weren't the ones who got squashed.

How would they like to be grounded and squashed at the same time?

The trouble with being squashed by a door is it makes you gulp.

And it makes your eyes bulge. Gabby said I looked like a goldfish. Mum said she should take a photo of me and send it to Freddy. Freddy is my goldfish. Was my goldfish. Kind of still is my goldfish. But we had to give him away. We gave him to Mrs Pike to look after. Mrs Pike is the lady next door. She's got a garden pond. That's where Freddy lives now.

I didn't want to give Freddy away. I wanted to keep him and teach him to talk, but the trouble was, he kept jumping out of his bowl.

The **trouble with jumping out of your bowl** when you're a goldfish is you end up on the carpet.

The **trouble with carpets** is they're nowhere near wet enough places for goldfish to live.

Flip knows why Freddy kept jumping out. Mum said it was because I kept feeding him live ants. She reckoned Freddy must have got live ants in his pants and all that wriggling must have made him want to keep jumping out of his bowl.

Trouble is, goldfish don't wear pants.

I think Freddy kept jumping out of his bowl because he thought he was a dolphin. When he was living in the sea before he came to our house, he must have met some dolphins who showed him how to do dolphin tricks.

If I was a goldfish, I'd much rather be a dolphin because dolphins are by far the best fish around. Dolphins know how to stand on their tails without sinking, and they can balance balls on their nose and even jump through hoops. Without ever landing on a carpet.

Freddies can't. That's **the trouble with goldfish who'd rather be dolphins**. They can't do tricks without falling out of their bowl.

Even if you've got quite a big bowl with weed and gravel in and everything.

The **trouble with weed and gravel and everything** is you have to keep it clean. Otherwise the water in your goldfish bowl goes green.

We came back from holiday once and you could hardly see Freddy. Mum said his water looked like pea soup, which is the worst kind of soup in the world.

Mum said the suitcases would have to wait, and before we'd even unpacked she put Freddy in a saucepan of clean water and then wiped all the green stuff off his bowl with a cloth.

I wanted to have a bath with

Freddy because it would be much more fun for him than a saucepan, but Mum wouldn't let me. Which isn't fair because I was really dirty after our holiday and really really needed a bath with Freddy.

If you have baths with goldfish, you can make hoops with your fingers for them to jump through and teach them tricks that even dolphins don't know!

But Mum said NO. Under NO circumstances am I allowed any alive fish in the bath with me at any time. Not Freddy. Not any goldfish. Not even a very small tadpole. Oo-er . . . Sorry – I just need to go somewhere again! . . .

CHAPTER 7

The **trouble with tadpoles** is mine never hatched.

The ones at school did. They were in a big jar on the window ledge in Mrs Donovan's class and they hatched all right. And grew legs. And ate bacon.

Mine didn't. The ones in my bucket just stayed like dots. Mum says I shouldn't have put the ham and live ants in until they'd hatched. But I thought if they saw the ham and live ants, they would get hungry and then they would want to hatch quicker. But the ham went mouldy and the ants crawled out. Then the water went smelly. And the dots just stayed like dots. That's the **trouble with frogspawn dots**. Sometimes they don't know what they're meant to do when you put them in a bucket.

The **trouble with buckets** is the more you fill them, the heavier they get.

When buckets are really heavy, you can hardly carry them at all. Heavy buckets do things they're not meant to do. Which isn't your fault. One day I was helping my mum clean the car and I filled our big red bucket with soapy water. Actually I put the water in first with a hose and then I put some bubble bath in afterwards.

Mum didn't know I was using bubble bath. She thought I was using normal car bath. But I thought the suds would be better if I used bubble bath. And they were. But the **trouble with suds** is they get really sudsy and grow and grow until all you can see is suds, and you can't see how much water is in the bucket.

Which isn't your fault. So when you try to lift the bucket and pour it on the car, the water goes the wrong way and spills all over you. Which isn't your fault either. It's the suds' fault. My mum said it wasn't the suds' fault at all. It was my fault, and if I ever use bubble bath on the car again, she will make me pay for some new bubbles out of my pocket money. Which isn't fair or my fault.

The **trouble with pocket money** is Mum never gives me enough.

I'd like to see Mum buy all the sweets she needs with only the pocket money I get. If you ask me, my pocket money should be at least a hundred— Sorry, got to go again!!!!

CHAPTER 8

The **trouble with tummy trouble** is you never know when you'll have to run to the loo!

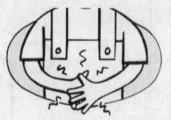

One minute you feel all right and then the next minute your bottom tells you to run up the stairs as fast as you can.

. . .

. . .

It's all my mum's fault I've got tummy trouble.

If she gave me a hundred pounds a week for my pocket money instead of 50p, I wouldn't have run out of money, or got tummy trouble or got grounded. That's the **trouble with having pocket money that isn't enough**: it gets you into trouble. Including tummy trouble.

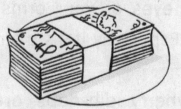

If you ask me, my pocket money should be at least a hundred pounds a week. No – a day. Actually, a minute. Then I'd be able to buy all the sweets I need without them ever running out.

My mum says that I should suck more and crunch less. Then my sweets would last much longer. It's all right for her. She can control her teeth. I can't. No children can. You have to be at least twenty-fiveish before you can control your teeth. Or your eyes or your arms or your fingers. Especially if it's a strawberry dib-dab.

Strawberry dib-dabs are totally my favourite sweets. The lolly bit tastes all strawberryyyeee and the sherbet feels all lovely and tingly and

fizzy on your tongue. No children can control their teeth when they're eating strawberry dib-dabs. No children called Daisy anyway. If you're eating a strawberry dib-dab and your name is Daisy, then you just have to crunch.

The **trouble with crunching** is, after four or five bites the lolly is always gone.

That's because lollies are always too small.

I tried really hard to suck a sweet once, but in the end my teeth made me crunch. That's the **trouble with not being about twenty-fiveish**.

You just can't control your teeth, however hard you try.

If after about five crunches you haven't got any bits of lolly stuck in your teeth, then the only thing you'll have left is the stick. The **trouble with lolly sticks** is you can't eat them.

If you ask me, you should be able to eat the lolly stick too. If you ask me, all lolly sticks should be made out of more lolly, so that you can eat them all the way down. That's the **trouble with people who make lollies**.

They don't understand how to make good sticks.

They don't know how to put more sherbet in the packet either. Whenever I open my dib-dab packets and look inside, there's always too

42

much air. Even before I've dipped in my lolly, there's loads more room for sherbet. About ten times more at least.

The **trouble with air** is you can't eat it.

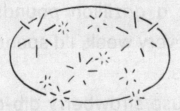

The **trouble with sherbet** is it dissolves too quickly and then turns into air.

And that's without even the slightest bit of crunching.

My mum says I should buy gobstoppers with my pocket money instead of strawberry dib-dabs. But I'd rather buy dib-dabs any day. If I had a gazillion pounds pocket money every week, I'd spend it all on dib-dabs.

Because strawberry dib-dabs are sooooooooooooooooo nice.

Strawberry dib-dabs are tooooooo ooooooooooooooooooooooooo nice.

You can't blame me if they're soooooooooo nice and tooooooooo ooo nice.

It's not my fault if they're lllllllllllll llllllllllllllllllllllllllllllllllllllllooooooooooo ooooooooooooooooooooooovvvvvvvvv vvvvvvvvvvvvvvvvvvvvvveeeeeeee eeeeeeeeeeeeeeeeeellllllllllllllllllllllllllll lllllllyyyyyyyyyyyyyyyyyyyyyyyyyyyyyyy yyyyyyyyyyyyyyyyyyyyyyyyy.

It's not my fault my pocket money had run out. Or that I had no money at all to buy sweets.

You can't blame me if someone dropped a half-sucked strawberry dib-dab on the pavement outside the shops.

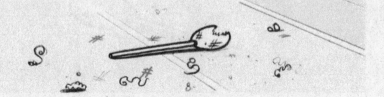

All I did was see it.

. . .

Pick it up off the pavement.

. . .

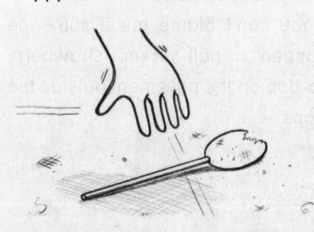

Put it in my mouth . . .

. . .

And eat it . . .

Excuse me – I need to go to the loo again!

CHAPTER 9

The **trouble with germs** is they're invisible.

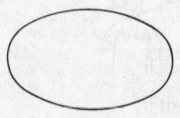

Germius Pavementius

Well, they're either invisible or they're red. Whatever they are, you definitely can't even slightly see them when they're on a half-sucked strawberry dib-dab.

So you can't even slightly blame

me, because invisible is as small as small things get.

In fact it's smaller than that. Invisible is totally teensy.

You'd need a greenfly's eyes to see something that was invisible.

Which absolutely isn't my fault. I mean, sometimes I can't even see the dirty socks on my bedroom floor! And they're LOADS bigger than germs.

I'm telling you, the only thing I could see on that dib-dab was some sherbet. And a bit of dirt which I picked off with my fingers. So how was I to know it had germs on it?

Germius Pavementius
magnified a zillion times

Anyway, I'd licked all the germs off before my mum even grabbed me.

My mum was really really reaaaa aaaaaaaaaaaaaaaaaaaaaaaaaaaa llyyyyyy cross with me when she came out of the butcher's. In fact her face was nearly redder than the dib-dab.

She said she saw me do what I did through the window of the shop but couldn't run out because she was still paying for the sausages.

That's the **trouble with sausages**.

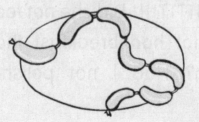

If they didn't take so long to pay for, I wouldn't have had time to put the dib-dab in my mouth.

When Mum grabbed me, she told me to spit whatever it was right out, right now. But she was too late. I was already on my fourth crunch.

"What will people think!" Mum said. "What WERE you thinking of!" she said. Had I gone mad? How could I possibly even think of picking up a dirty disgusting germ-covered sweet off the floor? And EATING IT? EATING ITTTT!!!! Did she not feed me? Had I not had breakfast that very morning? Had I not polished off

a boiled egg and soldiers AND two slices of toast and jam? Or had I had an argument with a witch while she was in the butcher's and been turned into a dustbin on legs?

I wasn't too sure what to say. I thought of asking for some more pocket money, but decided maybe this wasn't the time. So I didn't say anything at all. In any case, it wasn't even a whole dib-dab. It was only a half-sucked one with hardly any sherbet on it. So what was all the fuss about?

The **trouble with not saying anything at all** is it leaves lots of space for other people to say things.

My mum told me off ALL the way home in the car, and then when we got home, she told our neighbour Mrs Pike what I'd done.

Mrs Pike told Tiptoes too and then asked me if I thought Freddy would ever pick up a dirty fish flake from the floor of her pond. Before I could even answer, she told me, "NO HE MOST CERTAINLY WOULD NOT! Not if it was the last fish flake in the world."

Then my nanny and grampy came round to our house to lend Mum their step ladder. When they heard what I'd done, they weren't very pleased with me either. They said that even if they were in the war, when there were no sweets, they still wouldn't have picked a dirty sweet up off the pavement. Which doesn't make sense because if there were no sweets, how could one end up on the floor?

That's the **trouble with really old people**. Sometimes they don't know what they're saying.

Then, just my rotten luck: my Auntie Sue rings up to tell us about her new plasma green telly. Mum tells her about the dib-dab and then hands the phone to me. That's the **trouble with telephones**.

Some people just never stop talking.

Auntie Sue told me all about pavements and then all about germs. She said that once germs get inside your tummy, there's no telling what they can do. Especially if they're pavement germs. Pavement germs can give you diseases and tummy aches and headaches and temperatures. She said germs are like mini monsters. They've got ten heads and fifty eyes and twelve mouths with purple tongues and they love getting inside you so that they can do horrible things to you. Because germs are nasty. Germs are horrible. Germs are out to get you.

No wonder they hide on half-sucked strawberry dib-dabs — Oops, here I go again . . .

CHAPTER 10

Mum sent me to bed early last night. She said children who eat germy dib-dabs don't deserve to stay up late, even if it is a Friday. Even if there is no school in the morning.

But who cares anyway? I totally wanted to go to bed early yesterday. And double anyway, I had a new comic to read.

The **trouble with comics** is you only get a free gift on the front cover.

I think comics would be much better if you got free gifts on all the pages on the inside too. Then you wouldn't need to look at the comic. You could just play with the free toys.

I got some fly vision glasses in my last comic. When I put them on, they made everything in my bedroom look weird. Every time I looked at one thing it looked like a hundred things. I wore them in the sweet shop last Tuesday and they made even gobstoppers look great.

When I let Gabby try my glasses on in her garden, she said it wasn't fly vision. It was alien vision.

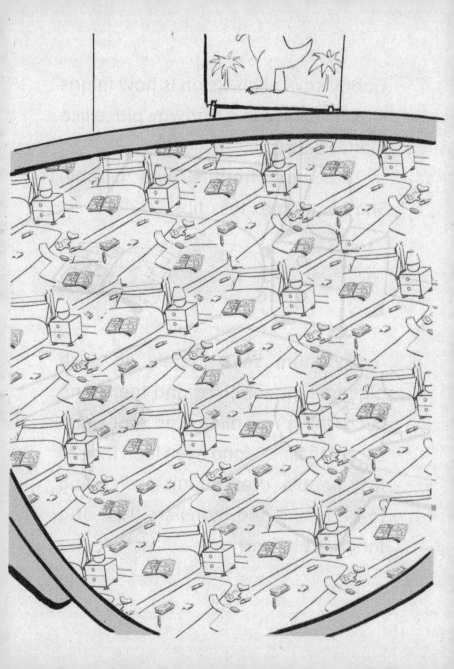

Gabby says alien vision is how things look if you live in a faraway place like planet Blerg.

That's the **trouble with Gabby**. She sometimes tells fibs.

My mum says there's no such place as planet Blerg and there's no such thing as aliens or monsters. Except in films – and even then they're just people dressed up pretending to be aliens and monsters. Like at a fancy-dress party.

That's the **trouble with films**.

They pretend to be real but they're not.

Last Halloween I went to a fancy-dress party and dressed up as a ghost! Ghosts aren't real either. They're just small children with sheets on.

I didn't like being a ghost at first because I couldn't see where I was going. When my mum turned my sheet round, it was much better

because then I could see out of the holes. And I could breathe.

Harry Bayliss who's in my class at school went to the party dressed as a hooley-hooley man with real fake blood and vampire fangs, but Vicky Carrow hit him on the head with her hooley-hooley stick. It wasn't a real hooley-hooley stick – it was a cucumber. Hooley-hooley men aren't real either by the way.

Except they do do real tears.

Harry Bayliss's dad came to collect him and all the monsters and ghosts were told to stop running around like loony ticks.

Vicky Carrow asked me if she could hide her cucumber up my sheet but I told her I needed both hands to eat my sandwiches.

That's the **trouble with party sandwiches**: if you don't take three or four all at once, other children will take all the nice ones.

Billy Laine said he had real bat's blood in his sandwiches. But it wasn't. It was raspberry jam.

So Vicky hit him on the head too.

And then she poked Jenny Pearson in the back for having a witch's nose.

Vicky Carrow's hooley-hooley stick got taken away in the end.

Actually, so did Vicky Carrow.

The **trouble with ghost sheets** is they make you ever so hot.

I was really sweating by the time my mum came to collect me. When I took it off outside by the car, my face went all cold in the fresh air.

Mum jumped when I took my sheet off, and pretended I was more scary without my sheet on. I only smiled a bit. I didn't laugh, because she's done that joke before.

When I got home after the party, I couldn't get to sleep, but when I did, I had a dream about skeletons. Which definitely are real because I saw one in an actual book at school once. Everything in school books has to be real. It's the law.

Anyway, in my dream four skeletons were chasing me!!!! And they were bouncing on big cucumbers like pogo sticks and trying to catch me!

It was really scary but there was nothing I could do, because the **trouble with bad dreams** is you always have to fall over before you can wake up.

But the more I tried to fall over, the more I stayed up. And the closer the skeletons got!

In the end I just closed my eyes and jumped . . .

My mum jumped too when I landed in her bed. She said she was right in the middle of a really nice dream about a handsome prince, who was just about to give her his phone number, when I had woken her up and made him drop his pen.

Which did make me laugh and smile a bit, and forget about the skeletons, because I hadn't heard that joke before. Hold on, I think I need to go to the loo again . . .

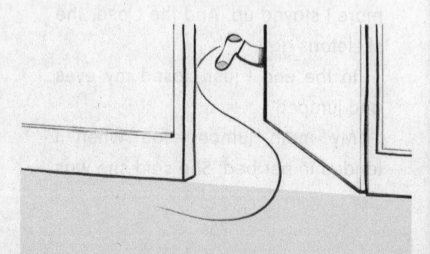

STILL CHAPTER 10

Actually no, I don't. I just thought I did. I'm OK.

In fact I think I'm beginning to feel a bit better!

Last night after I was sent to bed I didn't have any dreams at all. My tummy was too busy gurgling.

The **trouble with gurgles** is they sound really loud when they're your own gurgles. Especially if they're germ gurgles.

Germ gurgles are much more gurglier than normal gurgles.

By the time I'd thrown all my toys at the wall last night, and finished looking at my comic, and pulled all the whiskers off my rabbit (don't worry, he's a toy), my tummy sounded like it was a growling wolf.

When it was evening, Mum came up and pulled my curtains and told me never to pick anything up off the floor again apart from all my toys in the morning. Then she sat on my bed and listened.

She said my tummy sounded like a witch's pot and that trouble was brewing. And she said I only had myself to blame. She said if I hadn't been so naughty and put that dirty sweet in my mouth and eaten it, none of this would have happened.

That's the **trouble with mums**.

In the end, they're always right. And I'm wrong – I do need to go again . . .

CHAPTER 11

The **trouble with loo rolls** is they always run out when you don't want them to.

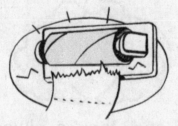

When I ran to the loo the first time last night, I went past Mum's bedroom really really quietly.

That way, she wouldn't know the dib-dab germs had got me.

And that way, in the morning I could pretend there never were any germs on that dib-dab. So then Mum would feel really bad about telling me off in the first place. So would Nanny and Grampy and Auntie Sue and Mrs Pike and Tiptoes!!!!!

Trouble is, when I turned the light on in the bathroom, the loo roll was all gone, apart from the cardboard bit in the middle. And I couldn't use that because . . . well I couldn't. And anyway, I always save that bit for Gabby's hamster. Gabby's hamster loves eating empty loo rolls.

So I had no choice.

"MUM, THERE'S NO LOO ROLL!"
I had to shout.

"WAKE UP! I NEED SOME LOO ROLL,"
I had to shout again.

The **trouble with shouting when someone's asleep** is they don't always hear you.

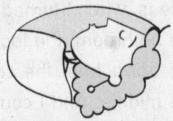

So then you have to shout louder and LOUDER, and kick the side of the bath with your feet too.

"MUM! MUM! THE DIB-DAB GERMS HAVE GOT ME. I'VE GOT TUMMY

TROUBLE!!!! HELP!!!!!!!!!!!" I had to shout at the top of my voice.

The **trouble with waking my mum up** is she doesn't really like it.

The **trouble with waking my mum up when she's in a bad mood**

is she REALLY doesn't like it.

I can tell because usually, when there's something wrong with me in the night, my mum pretends to keep her eyes open and rubs my back. But not last night. At least not when she came into the bathroom the first time.

The first time she came to see me, she folded her arms and tapped her toes on the bathroom floor and said, "You see, Daisy. You see what happens when you turn into a human dustbin. I told you tummy trouble was brewing. Goodness knows how many germs were on that lolly."

Luckily we had some more loo

rolls in the bathroom cupboard. Mum bought them yesterday before she went to the butcher's.

Trouble is, there are only twelve loo rolls in a pack.

Oo.

No.

Yes, no, yes.

Not sure . . .

See you in a min . . . !!!!!!!!!!!

CHAPTER 12

Phew!!

Good news at last! I didn't have to open loo roll number eleven!

In fact, I didn't have to go to the loo at all! Which means I must be getting better!

Which is a good job because the **trouble with brand-new loo rolls** is they can be really tricky to open.

A bit like cheese triangles.

Once, when I was hungry, I tried to make my own picnic, but I couldn't get the cheese out of the triangle at all. Until I squeezed it really really hard with both hands. Then all the cheese squidged out of one end, all over my fingers.

Mum says cheese triangles are really easy to open when you know how.

That's the **trouble with grown-ups**. They know everything.

At least they think they do.

I got most of the cheese out in the end but it didn't look anything like a triangle. Which made me really cross because triangles are my favourite shape. Then circles. Then squares.

I didn't fancy the cheese after that. So in the end I just ate the bread.

The **trouble with bread** is my mum never lets me cut it myself.

She says I'll have an accident

with the big knife and chop all my fingers off. Then I'll have to have a finger sandwich instead of a cheese sandwich, because good fingers shouldn't go to waste.

Anyway, how could I pick up a finger sandwich if all my fingers were inside the sandwich? She hasn't thought of that, has she?

The only things I'm allowed to cut in our house are craft paper and play-dough. With the red scissors.

I did cut Gabby's hair once when I was round her house, but she made me do it. It was definitely her idea, not mine.

The **trouble with Gabby's hair** is it fidgets a lot, so even if you're a really good hairdresser, it comes out wrong.

Gabby quite liked it from the front, but her mum only saw it from the back.

Playing hairdressers is banned in Gabby's house now. So are any games with scissors.

The **trouble with playing round Gabby's house** is she knows all the best places to hide. Whenever she

says, "COMING, READY OR NOT!" I'm never ready because I'm still looking for a good place to hide. I used to hide under her bed but she kept finding me, and now it's the same when I hide behind her lounge curtains.

Trouble is, whenever I say, "COMING READY OR NOT!" I can never find her anywhere. Not even when I've counted to a hundred in tens instead of ones.

Last time we played hide-and-seek at Gabby's house I was looking for her for ages. In the end I had to give up. And guess where she was?

In the laundry basket with all the smelly socks.

I told her that was cheating because I would never hide in a smelly place like that and so it didn't count and she'd have to hide again.

So she did and then I couldn't find her AGAIN! Even her mum couldn't find her.

That's because Gabby wasn't in the house, she was in the shed. Which is cheating too.

The **trouble with people who cheat at hide-and-seek** is they never admit it.

Especially Gabby. Sometimes, if she's been really cheating a lot, I tell her I'm never going to play with her again.

Trouble is, she always shares her sweets with me, and she's always really good fun too. It was Gabby who taught me how to jump up and down on the sofa and shout,

"Howzatcowpat!" at the same time. The first time we did it round her house on her mum's big leather sofa. Now we do it on my sofa too! Only when my mum's not looking though.

Actually. Thinking about it . . . Maybe I should have a little bounce on our sofa right now. Just to see if I really am getting better. I'll do it extra quietly and I'll whisper "Howzatcowpat" instead of shouting it . . . just in case Mum hears!

Why don't you have a go on your sofa too? This is how Gabby and me do it.

CHAPTER 13

Twenty whopping bounces and ten Howzatcowpats without laughing! That's really good! Gabby can never do more than six Howzatcowpats without laughing.

The **trouble with laughing** is it can make lemonade come out of your nose. Not when you're doing howzatcowpats – when you're in restaurants.

Once, when me and Gabby were at Pizza Heaven with my mum, Gabby stuck two marshmallow flumps in her ears and pulled a really funny face.

Trouble is, I'd only just taken a drink of my lemonade, so when I laughed, my lemonade didn't go down the right hole. It went up all the wrong holes instead. Then my nose started fizzing and my eyes started watering and my mouth started choking.

Well, sort of choking and laughing at the same time, which is a really hard thing to do.

In the end, my mum had to call a waitress to help her pat me on the back. They made me stand up at the table in front of everybody.

The **trouble with someone patting you on the back** is, if they don't do it hard enough, it doesn't do any good at all, and if they do it too hard, it makes you sound like a seal.

No one had ever heard a seal in Pizza Heaven before, so everyone stopped eating their pizzas and looked at me.

Then Gabby got two dough balls and pretended my eyes had popped out and fallen onto the table, which made me laugh even more.

And choke and splutter.

In the end the manageress came out and took me to the toilets and made me drink a load of water out of the tap. Mum had to rub my back for about ten minutes before we could go back to our table.

Flumps are banned when we go to Pizza Heaven now. And dough balls.

We're still allowed lemonade, but

only if we don't blow bubbles with our straws.

Which reminds me, I need to drink some more water. Mum says if I drink lots of water today, it will help flush all the dib-dab germs away.

Back in a minute!

CHAPTER 14

Have you ever blown bubbles in your lemonade with a straw? It sort of still works with water and it's quite good in milk. But lemonade's the best.

I tried to do it in a really thick milkshake once, but my mum told me to stop being silly.

The **trouble with being silly** is it can give you scabs.

Not silly with straws – silly with skipping ropes.

At school the other day Gabby and I were doing skipping with Liberty Pearce, except we weren't doing the skipping, Liberty was. Gabby and me were doing the rope.

Anyway, Liberty said she was the best skipper in the school and she said she was the fastest. So Gabby and I went faster with the rope because we thought Liberty wanted us to, but when we switched to super-speed, Liberty wasn't ready, so her legs got caught up in the rope and she fell over and scraped her knees. And she made holes in her tights and she got scabs.

Mrs Donovan said that Gabby and I had been very silly with the rope and that Liberty wasn't a kangaroo and couldn't possibly jump that fast or high. We had to write "We will not be silly with skipping ropes" ten times on a piece of paper during morning break the next day.

Another time Gabby and me were silly with the hosepipe in my garden. No one got scabs, but we did get told off by Mrs Pike. It was a really hot day and Mum had got the paddling pool out of the shed for Gabby and me to play in.

The **trouble with paddling pools** is you have to blow them up with a pump.

Trouble was, Mum couldn't find our pump so she had to do it with her mouth.

So while she was huffing and puffing and blowing, Gabby and me said we'd water the garden. Well we never actually said we'd water the garden, we just did it. While Mum wasn't looking.

First of all we watered the flowers because they looked really hot. Then we watered the grass, which was going a bit brown. Then we watered the shed, which was really brown.

Then we watered Tiptoes.

The **trouble with watering Tiptoes** is he's a cat.

Which means he doesn't like it. Which isn't our fault, because when we watered him, he looked like he really wanted to be watered. I mean, he was right in a really hot bit of sun, all stretched out, not moving even a little bit. Me and Gabby thought he was dying of thirst so we thought he really needed some water.

When the water went on him, he wasn't still any more. He jumped up and went higher than a kangaroo, right over the wall and back into Mrs Pike's garden.

Then Mrs Pike poked her head over the wall and looked at me and Gabby with a cross face and said, "WHO DID THAT TO TIPTOES? HE'S SOAKED!"

The **trouble with holding hose-pipes** is people can always tell which one did the squirting.

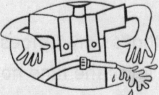

So I let go.

The **trouble with letting go of hosepipes** is you can't tell which way they are going to squirt. Which isn't your fault.

Mum said it *was* my fault though. When it squirted her, and made her dress all wet, she said playing with the hosepipe was a very silly thing to do. So did Mrs Pike.

I think that's why Tiptoes stays on the wall a lot of the time now.

Anyway, Mum was so wet she nearly didn't keep on blowing, but then she said that at least if Gabby and I were in the paddling pool, she would know where we were and what we were up to.

We weren't allowed to put the water in the paddling pool after that. Only Mum was.

The **trouble with paddling pool water** is it always gets dead bees floating on it.

Gabby says dead bees can still sting you, so you have to splash them out.

The **trouble with splashing dead bees out of your paddling pool** is it makes all the water go on the grass.

After three bees we only had a centimetre left.

Mum filled the paddling pool up again for us but said there would be no more after that. She said that water is precious and that if we use too much in our paddling pool, all the oceans will go down, including Mrs Pike's pond, which will be bad news for Freddy.

So the next time we got a bee in our water Gabby tried to splish it out instead of splash it out. Splishes are smaller than splashes.

Trouble is, she splished the dead bee onto her arm. If a dead bee stings you on the arm, your whole body can fall off, so Gabby went a bit loopy.

Luckily it fell off her arm onto the grass. So we managed to trap it under the big red bucket.

Gabby said she was really lucky

to be alive and if her whole body had fallen off, she would never have been able to ride her new bike again. Or do skipping. Mum brought the towels out after that.

Hang on. Where is Mum? I can't hear her in the kitchen and I can't hear her upstairs. Maybe she's in the garden – I'll just go and see.

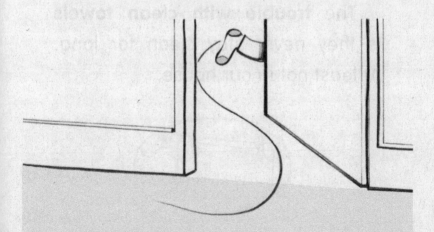

CHAPTER 15

Thought so. Mum's in the garden, hanging up the washing. She always does the washing on Saturday afternoon. She says if she does the washing on Saturdays, we can start the week with clean towels.

The **trouble with clean towels** is they never stay clean for long. At least not in our house.

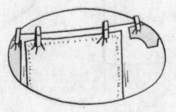

Mum says that the towels would stay clean a lot longer if I got all the dirt off BEFORE I dried myself. She says dirt doesn't wash itself off, it has to be rubbed or scrubbed off. One rub for normal dirt, three rubs for mud, five rubs for grass stains and about two hundred and seventy-three scrubs for snake poo.

I'm not joking. If you get snake poo on you, you are in BIG trouble. Believe me, I know!

The **trouble with snake poo** isn't so much the look of it, it's the STINK of it. It stinks like a hundred stink bombs.

And if it squirts on you, you'll never get it off. And that's just with a little snake, like Dylan Reeves's. Imagine if it was a massive python or something! Imagine the stink then!

Dylan Reeves lives three doors away at Number 38. He's two years older than me, but sometimes he asks me round to play.

It's really good at Dylan's. His mum and dad have got a hot tub in their back garden. And asparagus.

Dylan's bedroom is the best. He's got his own telly in it, and a PlayStation, and he used to have a snake called Shooter.

Shooter was a Colorado garter snake. He wasn't very long – about as long as from my fingers to my elbow – and he was sort of light brown with a stripy crisscrossy pattern.

He lived in Dylan's bedroom, in a tank with a really bright light and heat pads under the sawdust.

Most of the time I just looked at him through the glass, but one day Dylan let me hold him.

I wasn't scared or anything – Dylan thought I would be, but I wasn't. I've always wanted to hold a snake.

But the **trouble with holding snakes** is, without telling you or anything, they can poo on you just like that.

That's what Shooter did to me. I'd only been holding him for about a minute. I was looking at his tongue going in and out when he suddenly started to wriggle.

I tried to stop him from wriggling, but Dylan said I must have squeezed him too hard. Anyway, he pooed all over my hands. That's when I dropped him.

The **trouble** **with** **dropping** **snakes** is they are ten times worse than hosepipes.

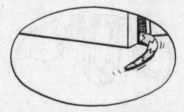

At least hosepipes stay still at one end. Snakes don't. They don't stay still at either end, they just wriggle across the carpet really fast and then disappear out of the door.

That's the last time we saw Shooter. At least that was the last time we saw his face. Dylan saw his tail disappear down a crack between some upstairs floorboards, but by the time his dad pulled the floorboard up with a big hammer, he was gone.

We did find five pence and a paperclip though.

Dylan was really upset. He'd only had Shooter a month. I was even more upset. I had snake poo all over me.

Dylan's dad said it wasn't poo, it was "musk". He said it's the same sort of thing that skunks spray on people when they feel threatened. That made me feel even worse! Now I had skunk poo on me!

I said sorry to Dylan for dropping his snake and went home after that.

My mum said she could smell me when I walked through the kitchen door, and when I made her smell my hand, she nearly fainted.

It took a whole bar of soap, some washing-up liquid, some disinfectant and a dishwasher tablet to get the smell off. Plus I rubbed all the fluff off TWO towels!

Next time I saw Dylan, I asked him if he'd found Shooter. He said he hadn't, but he hadn't given up looking. He said the central heating pipes under the floorboards might act like heat pads and keep him warm so Shooter still might be OK.

Dylan sleeps under his bed in a sleeping bag now. That way he can sleep with his ear pressed to the floor. That way if Shooter wriggles back in the night, Dylan will hear him.

I hope he finds Shooter one day. Stinky or not.

Oh dear.

I just gurgled . . .

Oh dear, I just gurgled again.

Now then . . .

Are those germ gurgles?

Or hungry gurgles?

I'm going to run to the loo just in case. Back in a minute!

CHAPTER 16

Fantastic news! It was a hungry gurgle! I must really be getting better!

I haven't had breakfast or lunch today, so no wonder I'm getting hungry gurgles.

My mum said drinking water would be all right, but for a while eating food wouldn't be a very good idea at all. She said she got up to rub my back seventy-three times last night and even if I tried to eat anything, it would probably go straight through me.

To be honest, I haven't felt even the slightest bit hungry till now. And even now I don't feel that hungry.

I was opening loo roll number eight this morning when Mum told me I was grounded. She said she didn't like grounding me, but because eating a sweet off the pavement was such a disgusting thing to do, I had to learn my lesson. Otherwise I might do it again. I s'pose she's right.

I promised her I would never ever EVER do it again. And I double promised I would never pick anything up off ANY floor again EVER EVER, except for the toys in my bedroom.

Then I triple promised that even if I saw a hundred strawberry dib-dabs lying on the pavement, still in their packets, with a PLEASE EAT ME sign next to them, I still wouldn't pick them up. Which was a bit of a fib, but I really didn't want her to ground me. And then, for luck, I four times definitely promised I wouldn't even go into a sweet shop again, which is a huge fib, but it was worth a try. I said if I ever saw a sweet shop again, I'd shut my eyes and walk straight past. Cross my heart, hope to die.

But I was still grounded. That's

the **trouble with my mum when she's really cross**. When she says something, she means it.

I suppose at least when Gabby called for me earlier, Mum didn't tell her what I'd done. The **trouble with telling Gabby** is she might tell someone at school.

Like Jack Beechwhistle. If Jack Beechwhistle finds out I've eaten a germy dib-dab, he'll tell my whole class.

And he'll call me names, like Germbelly or Dib-dab Gob. That's the **trouble with Jack Beechwhistle**, he's really good at calling people names.

In fact he's the best in the school.

But I think he's an idiot with knobs on.

So's Fiona Tucker. She sits next to me in class. I used to sit next to Gabby, but Mrs Donovan moved me because Gabby talked too much.

Last month it was "Lend to a Friend Week" at school, so I lent Fiona Tucker my kaleidoscope to play with. And guess what?

She broke it.

She said it wasn't her fault. She said she was walking along the street with her dad, looking at all the different patterns it could make, when she walked into a lamp post.

I was really cross with her when

she told me. I told her she should have been looking where she was going, but she said you can't see lamp posts through a kaleidoscope. You can only see pretty patterns.

I said it was still her fault, because she shouldn't have borrowed my kaleidoscope if she was going to crunch it into a lamp post or anything made of concrete. I was soooooooooo cross with her, I nearly asked Jack Beechwhistle to think up some really horrible names to call her.

Except she got a black eye. It was red to start with, then it went blue, then it went black.

So I didn't think it would be very kind to call her names on top.

That's the **trouble with black eyes**: they make you feel sorry for people. Even if they've broken your toys.

Not if they're boxers on the telly though.

If you're a boxer on the telly, then it serves you right if you get a black eye, because you shouldn't be fighting someone in the first place. And you definitely shouldn't be doing hard punches.

That's the **trouble with boxers**. Black eyes are definitely their own fault.

Unless, I suppose, you're a boxer who's walked into a lamp post, with a kaleidoscope.

Anyway, Mum said Fiona Tucker was a very lucky girl, because if she'd taken my kaleidoscope to the seaside, she might have walked off a cliff with it and fallen miles down into the sea or onto the rocks.

Then she'd have had a lot more than a black eye. She'd have had two black eyes at least.

And anyway, Fiona's dad said he'd buy me a new one. But he hasn't yet.

But he said he would.

. . .

Sometimes, like for instance when I've been told off, I wish I had a dad.

Trouble is, I haven't.

. . .

My dad is dead.

. . .

Because he died.
When I was little.

The **trouble with not having a dad because he died when you were little** is sometimes I wonder what he was like.

Mum says my dad was the best dad in the world, but he would still have told me off if I'd been naughty.

I suppose he definitely would have told me off if I'd eaten a germy dib-dab.

But I can't remember.

That's the **trouble with not**

being little any more. You can't
remember.

. . .

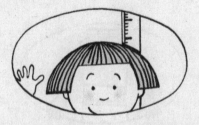

However hard you try, you just
can't remember.

. . .

And your clothes stop fitting.
Apart from your socks, 'cos socks
are stretchy.

The **trouble with growing** is your favourite clothes don't grow with you.

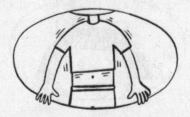

A year ago, my favourite yellow T-shirt used to come down right over my belly button, but it doesn't any more. Neither does my disco top with the stars on.

Mum says I'll be borrowing her clothes soon!

Another **trouble with growing** is the saddle on your bike won't go up any higher either. Gabby got a new bike for her last birthday so her legs look normal when she rides.

My legs look silly on my bike because my knees go too high when I turn the pedals. So I don't ride my bike much any more.

My mum got some spanners out of the garage last week and tried to make my saddle go right up as high as it would go, but when she pulled the saddle up, it came right off the bike! Then it took us ages to get it back on. So now I just leave my bike in the garage.

Mum says if I'm good, I can have a new second-hand bike for my next birthday.

Trouble is, my birthday isn't for three whole months.

Last year I got a remote control car for my birthday. It was white.

To start off with.

The **trouble with remote control cars** is they don't do as they are told.

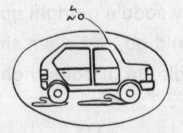

If you try and make them go one way, they go the other, plus if you drive them through muddy puddles, they conk out.

Mum says I shouldn't have driven my car through a puddle. She says it makes the battery wet. That's the **trouble with batteries**. They don't like getting wet.

When I brought my car indoors, she said, "OH DAISY, WHAT HAVE YOU DONE? YOU'VE ONLY HAD IT TWO

MINUTES! IT'S A CAR, DAISY, NOT A HOVERCRAFT. WHAT WERE YOU THINKING OF?"

I said submarines.

Mum said, "GO AND FETCH THE PAPER TOWELS."

After we dried the battery, it still didn't work, so Mum said she would take it back to the shop and complain.

So she did. But that didn't work either because the man behind the counter didn't believe what Mum said.

"PUDDLES! WHAT PUDDLES?" said my mum. "This car hasn't been anywhere near a puddle! IT

HASN'T EVEN BEEN OUT OF DOORS!"

The man said we must have a very swampy carpet because when he opened the boot and shook it, dirty water came out all over his jumper.

I don't do remote control driving any more. I just do parking. Which isn't anywhere near as much fun.

Luckily, Gabby says I can have lots of fun on her new bike, as long as I promise not to fall off and bend the wheels. Or drink all the drink in her drinks bottle. Trouble is, she puts orange squash in her drinks bottle, which is one of my favourite drinks in the whole wide world.

Hold on, I can smell sausages
. . . sausages are my favourite meat
in the world!
Back in a minute . . .

CHAPTER 17

I was right! It's sausages for tea. With mashed potato, gravy and corn on the cob! If I'm well enough, Mum says I can have some when they're ready, but only if I'm feeling totally better.

Actually I really do feel much better! And hungrier! No gurgles, or anything. I really really think the dib-dab germs might have gone away.

Mmmmmmm . . . there's only one way to be really really sure though . . .

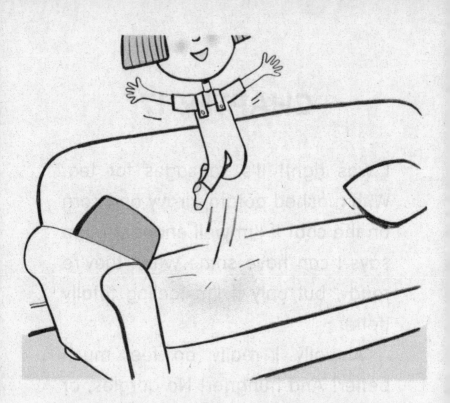

I'll do a hundred Howzatcowpats
on the sofa . . .

Start counting . . . Now! . . . I'll let
you know how I get on.

CHAPTER 18

200 bounces! 101 Howzatcowpats!!

And I didn't even want to run to the loo once!

No gurgles either!

I'm better! I must be better!

I wish Gabby would come and call for me now.

Trouble is, I'm still grounded.

Even though I'm back to normal, I've still got nothing to do. I've still got no one to play with, and nowhere to go.

Being grounded is even worse when there's nothing wrong with you.

I wish I could magic myself to a faraway place, where there's loads of things to do. A place like you see on the telly or in holiday magazines . . .

Like Cornwall!

Trouble is, I don't know any words that rhyme with Cornwall either. So I can't do the magic spell.

Me and Mum went to Cornwall for our holiday last year. We stayed in a place called Mevawishywashy, or something like that, and it was so far away, by the time we got there it was dark!

Mum says that's because we should have left earlier. She said when you drive somewhere as far away as Cornwall, you need to get up really early to avoid all the traffic.

Trouble is, I couldn't find my colouring book for the journey, or my other welly. And then when we got on to the big road, we had to go back for my crab line. Otherwise I wouldn't have been able to catch any crabs.

The **trouble with crabs** is they nip.

Especially when you try and get them into your bucket.

One day, me and Mum were sitting on the harbour wall with my crab line when this really big crab grabbed my piece of fish. Mum said to count to ten before I lifted my line, otherwise he might fall off. So I did and he didn't, but when we tried to get him off the fish and into the bucket, his claws bent right back and tried to nip us. And forwards and sideways.

Mum held him over our bucket and tried to shake him off, but he still wouldn't let go. Then he did.

Not over the bucket – right by my leg! So I panicked, and then my welly fell off into the sea, which wasn't my fault, and then the crab fell into the sea too, and my mum kicked over the bucket, and then all our other crabs escaped too and fell back into sea with the big crab!

That's where my mum says they all live now. In my welly.

The **trouble with welly shops in Cornwall** is most of them only sell yellow ones.

Gabby's wellies are green with a frog face, but they didn't have any like those. In the end I got a red pair. They pinch my toes a bit but I didn't tell Mum or I would have had to have yellow again.

The **trouble with yellow wellies** is Paddington Bear wears them.

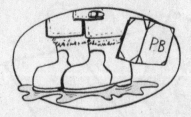

Rebecca Isaacs wore yellow wellies in the playground once and Jack Beechwhistle called her Paddington all day!

That's why my wellies will never be yellow again.

Which reminds me, if Mum un-grounds me tomorrow, I'm definitely going to need my red wellies.

Especially if we make it a really really big mud trap with lots of water and extra mud.

I won't be a moment. I just need to ask Mum where my wellies are . . .

CHAPTER 19

Mum says my sausages will be ready in five minutes. And she says my wellies are in the shed. Apparently they are still drying out after my last school trip.

The **trouble with school trips** is they should tell you to take a change of clothes. Especially if there are going to be ducks there.

There were loads of ducks at Lime Tree Farm.

The **trouble with the ducks at Lime Tree Farm** is the ones with green heads are far too greedy.

Which means the other ducks hardly get a chance to eat any of the bread that you throw at them.

Gabby and I had saved every last bit of our packed lunch especially for the ducks. Apart from our chocolate biscuit and our tangerines. Gabby said the ones with green heads were daddy ducks. She said if you wanted to feed the mummy ducks and the baby ducks, you had to throw your bread really close to their beaks so the daddy ducks couldn't get to it first.

The **trouble with throwing bread at ducks** is it's really hard to get it in the right place.

Especially if your bread has got strawberry jam on with no pips.

Every time I threw a piece of my sandwiches to a mummy or a baby duck, it went in the wrong place and a daddy duck ate it.

One of the baby ducklings was really cute. He was yellow and fluffy instead of brown and fluffy like all the other ones, and I really wanted him to have a piece of my sandwich without crust on. But even when I pointed to where I was going to throw it, he couldn't get there in time.

If I threw to the left, a daddy duck got it. If I threw to the right, a daddy duck got it. If I did a long throw, a daddy duck got it, and if I just dropped it down the edge, a daddy duck got it.

In the end I got really cross. After about twenty throws, Gabby's sandwiches had completely run out and I only had one piece of my sandwich left.

It was a really nice piece too, with no crust on and oodles of strawberry jam inside.

And I REALLY wanted the yellow fluffy duckling to have it.

And then I fell in. I was kind of hoping it was Jack Beechwhistle's fault, but it wasn't.

I was kind of leaning over the pond trying to get the yellow baby duck to come to me when a load of daddy ducks all came over to me at the same time.

I tried to shoo them away but when I waved them away with my arm, I kind of lost my balance and fell into the pond.

It wasn't very deep, but it was really wet, and the mud at the bottom was really yucky. And my school uniform got soaked.

Gabby screamed, the ducks swam away really fast and Mr Cheetham jumped in to save me.

When everyone realized the water wasn't very deep, they all started laughing. Gabby said they weren't laughing at me, they were laughing at Mr Cheetham. The water only came up to his knees and he could have reached me from the side if he'd wanted.

Mr Cheetham lifted me out of the pond and carried me back to the school bus. Mrs Donovan made me dry myself on a picnic blanket and then I had to empty my wellies onto the grass beside the school bus.

The worst thing was, I wasn't allowed to sit next to Gabby on the way home. Mrs Donovan made me sit at the front of the bus next to the coach driver all the way back to school.

I never did figure out which duck got my last bit of sandwich. I hope it was the baby yellow one. Don't s'pose it was though.

Apart from greedy ducks, Lime Tree Farm is a really good place to go for a school trip. You should ask your teacher to take you. They have loads of animals to look at, including real pigs that are going to turn into actual bacon.

Fiona Tucker says that making

pigs into bacon is cruel, but Gabby said that different animals on farms have different jobs to do. A farm dog's job is to bark at the sheep, a horse's job is to pull wagons, a chicken's job is lay eggs for breakfast, a cow's job is to make milk for cups of tea and a pig's job is to turn into bacon.

We never did work out what a duck's job is though.

I'll go and ask my mum.

CHAPTER 20

Mum says a duck's job is to stay in the water on a school trip and my job is to stay out of the water on a school trip.

She also says my sausages are ready, so I can have another job.

Washing my hands for dinner.

Sigh.

It's a germ thing.

Sorry about this – I'll see you up at the dining table in a couple of minutes.

That's if you don't mind watching me eat.

CHAPTER 21

Numyumyumyum yum yum nyum
yum yumm yummy yumnum yum
num yum nyum nuyyum yum yum
yummy yum nyum – sorry again . . .
   The **trouble with trying to
finish a story with your mouth full**
is nothing you say makes any sense.
All your words are too full of sausage
or sweetcorn, gravy or mash.

Don't worry. I'm going to ask Spiggy, my pet money spider, to tell the rest of the story for me. He's sitting on my shoulder right now.

Say hello, Spiggy.

"Hi!"

Do you mind telling the rest of the story for me, Spig?

"Not at all!"

Otherwise my sausages will get cold.

"Leave it to me!"

CHAPTER 22

Daisy smiled sweetly at the most handsome money spider in the world (that's me!) and tucked hungrily into her dinner.

Sorry, can you read the words OK when they're this small? OK, I'll shout!

As she raised a fork full of sausage and mash to her lips, her mum leaned across the table and placed a hand on her arm.

"Any more gurgles?" she asked, a little anxious that the dib-dab germs might come back, and more than a little concerned that they only had one loo roll left if they did.

Daisy shook her head, and popped another forkful into her mouth.

"Numyum yum yum yumnuyum yum yum," she smiled.

"Well, I hope you've learned your lesson today, Daisy," said her mum. "You know I really hate grounding you, but sometimes needs must."

Daisy paused in mid-munch. She'd never understood what "needs must" meant but kind of figured it was something that mums just have to do.

"It's OK," said Daisy, "I know picking a germy dib-dab up off the pavement and then eating it was a disgusting thing to do. I have learned my lesson and I don't blame you for grounding me. I'll never do it again. Ever! I promise!!"

Daisy's mum sighed with relief. "That's very good to hear, Daisy. Very good indeed! No one will be happier than me to have a germ-free Daisy back in action again!"

Daisy swallowed a big mouthful of gravy and mash and then raised her eyebrows hopefully.

"So does that mean I'm not grounded any more?" she said, hoping she might be able to start work on the mud trap that evening."

Daisy's mum shook her head. "You're still grounded until the end of the day," she said, "but after today you can play outside again."

Daisy sighed a smallish sigh and then began making plans for Sunday. "So Gabby can come round to play first thing tomorrow?" she asked.

"As long as it's not too first

thing," said Daisy's mum. "I do like to have a lie-in on a Sunday."

Daisy smiled to herself and set about polishing off her plate.

"Mum," she said, gobbling up the last piece of sweetcorn and slurping down the last dribble of orange squash. "Do you know any words that rhyme with 'hippopotamus'?"

Daisy's mum swallowed, frowned and then leaped up from the table and squealed.

"TIPTOESGOTAMOUSE!" she squeaked, pointing in horror at the French windows behind Daisy.

Daisy wheeled round in her chair and stared in the direction of her mum's pointing finger.

There, beside the flowerbed in a pool of evening sunlight, towered Tiptoes. His back was arched, his tail was looped and he was dabbing something wickedly with his paw.

Daisy's mum covered her eyes again as the mouse suddenly twitched, sending Tiptoes into a somersault of excitement.

Daisy sprang up from her chair and raced out of the kitchen door into the back garden.

Grounded or not, if there was a mouse in trouble in her garden, then she was going to be the one to rescue it!

"Scat!" said Daisy. "Shoo, you nasty cat! Leave that mouse alone!"

Tiptoes looked up from the flowerbed in the direction of the kitchen door. His whiskers wilted at the sight of Daisy hurtling across the garden towards him. The very thought of bangs from spade handles and squirts from hosepipes sent him catapulting over the wall.

Daisy's eyes flashed angrily

from the top of Mrs Pike's wall and then anxiously to the flowerbed directly below.

Suddenly her eyes widened and a huge smile crept across her face.

"SHOOTER!!!" she squealed, dropping onto her knees.

It wasn't a mouse that Tiptoes had found basking in the late evening sunshine. It was a snake.

A Colorado garter snake, to be exact!

Daisy snatched Shooter up from the flowerbed, hugged him to her chest and ran back into the kitchen.

"Look, Mum, it's SHOOTER! He's alive!" she shouted, careful not to squeeze too hard. "He's been lost for ages and now I've found him again! Quick, find something for me to put him in before he starts to wriggle!"

Daisy's mum took a nervous step backwards in the direction of the kitchen drawer.

"We must take him back to Dylan right this minute!" beamed Daisy.

Daisy's mum held her best Tupperware bowl out at arm's length and then shuddered as Daisy lowered Shooter carefully inside.

"Dylan is going to be SOOOOOOOOO pleased to see him again!" chuckled Daisy, snapping the lid of the Tupperware bowl shut.

"PLEEEEAAAAAASSSSSSSE can we go and take Shooter back to Dylan right now?"

Daisy's mum frowned. She had been awake most of the night and it had been a long and tiring day. Although being grounded had been no fun for Daisy, it had certainly been no fun for Daisy's mum either.

Having a moping, frowning,

grumbling Daisy around the house all day was a bit like living with a small troll.

But rules were rules. Daisy was grounded and that should mean staying indoors, not scampering up the road to Number 38.

Daisy's mum looked at the Tupperware bowl and then deep into Daisy's pleading eyes.

"Very well, Daisy," she sighed, "but you're still grounded the moment you get back from Dylan's."

"It's a deal!" said Daisy, racing to the front door.

"I'll open it!" said her mum,

overtaking her in the hall. "I don't want you squashing yourself against the wall again!"

After a tug and a yank and a heave-ho, the front door sprang open and Daisy raced down the path.

When she returned home ten minutes later, she was a girl transformed. From a small troll to her usual bubbly self.

"Dylan was so pleased to see Shooter again, he nearly kissed me!" she gushed. "Shooter's back in his snake tank now, but Dylan's moved it down beside his bed so he can see him. Dylan sleeps under his bed all the time now. He says sleeping under the bed in a sleeping bag is totally cool. I think Dylan's totally cool too. Trouble is, he's a bit old for me."

Daisy's mum smiled and, with a flap of a tea towel, returned to the kitchen sink.

That's the **trouble with sausage and mash with sweetcorn and gravy.** The washing-up that comes with it.

And that's the trouble with this story. There isn't any more to tell.

So that's me done. Glad to be of service. I'm off to spin a web.

Be good, and remember: give spiders a break. You're the ugly-looking ones.

Actually there is a little bit more

to the story but it will happen at
bedtime, later.

BEDTIME, LATER

TIPTOESGOTAMOUSE!

That's the word I've been trying to think of all week! Mum said it in the kitchen earlier! Tiptoesgotamouse rhymes with "hippopotamus"! Now Gabby and I can write our magic spell!

I knew if I slept under my bed in a sleeping bag just like Dylan, the magic rhyming word would come into my head!

Mum said sleeping under the bed was silly, and that I should sleep under my covers like normal children. But the **trouble with normal children** is they don't have to write magic spells.

When Mum tucked me in, she made me promise I wouldn't get out of bed. She said, "If I find you asleep under the bed in the morning, Daisy, I'll pour orange squash on your cornflakes."

She was only joking. She wouldn't

dare pour orange squash on my cornflakes. At least I don't think she would.

Anyway, I'm bound to wake up before her tomorrow. She says she's so tired after rubbing my back all last night she'll probably sleep for about three hundred years.

She might even be asleep already.

"MUM!!!!! ARE YOU ASLEEP ALREADY YET??????!!!!!!"

Grunt, snuffle, yawwwwwwnnnn . . .

"NOT ANY MORE I'M NOT, DAISY!"

. . .

"MUMMM!! DO YOU BELIEVE IN MAGIC SPELLS?"

Grunt, snuffle, gasp . . . "DAISY, THE ONLY THING I BELIEVE IN IS AN EARLY NIGHT. NOW STOP TALKING AND GO TO SLEEP!"

. . .

"MUUUUMMMMMM! I'VE GOT THE RHYMING WORD I NEED FOR MY MAGIC SPELL."

. . .

"DAISY! WILL YOU PLEASE STOP TALKING AND GO TO SLEEP! THERE'S NO SUCH THING AS MAGIC SPELLS!"

. . .

"MUUUMMMMMM!!!! IF YOU'RE FRIGHTENED OF HIPPOPOTAMUSES,

YOU'D BETTER NOT GO INTO THE GARDEN TOMORROW!!!"

. . .

"AND IF YOU'RE FRIGHTENED OF GRUMPY MUMS WHO HAVEN'T HAD ANY SLEEP, DAISY, YOU'D BETTER NOT MAKE ANOTHER SOUND!!"

. . .

"I JUST THOUGHT I SHOULD TELL YOU ABOUT THE HIPPOPOTAMUS, THAT'S ALL."

. . .

"DAISY. WILL YOU PLEASE STOP TALKING AND GO TO SLEEP! THERE'S NO SUCH THING AS MAGIC SPELLS!"

. . .

Sigh. That's the trouble with eating a germy dib-dab, **being grounded, getting a runny tummy, feeling better and then trying to tell someone who hasn't had enough sleep about a cat called Tiptoes who's going to turn into a magic hippopotamus on the wall in the garden tomorrow** . . .

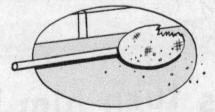

Somehow, they just don't believe you! The end, well, nearly . . .

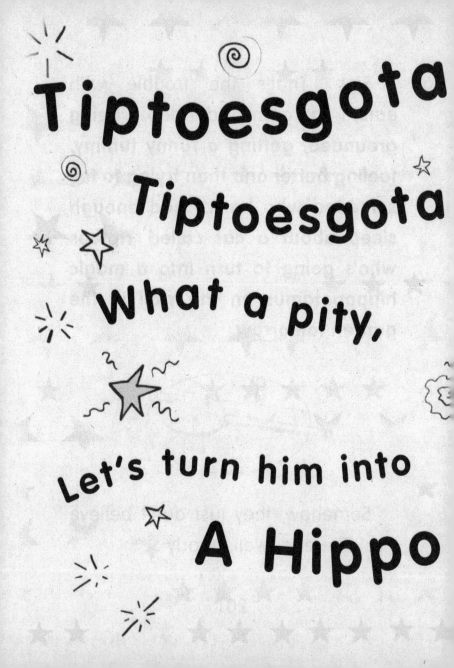

Tiptoesgota

Tiptoesgota

What a pity,

Let's turn him into

A Hippo

mouse!

mouse!

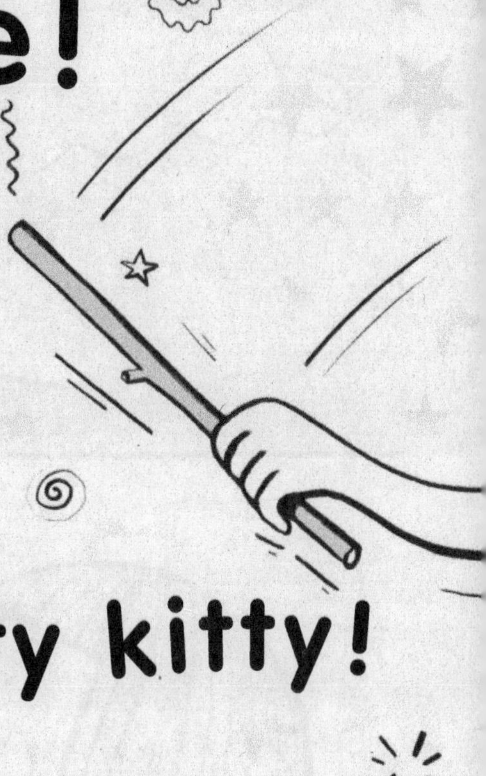

Naughty kitty!

potamus!

DAISY'S TROUBLE
INDEX

The trouble with . . .

Lolly sticks 41

 People who make
lollies 42

 Air 43

 Sherbet 43

 Germs 48

 Sausages 51

 Not saying anything
at all 54

 Really old people 58

A nod and a wink to
Colchester Zoo

DAISY

and the TROUBLE with

ZOOS

by Kes Gray

RED FOX

CHAPTER 1

The **trouble with zoos** is they shouldn't say things they don't mean. Especially on seven-year-olds' birthdays. If zoos say things they don't mean on a seven-year-old's birthday, then anything can happen. Which is why what happened today DID happen. Which ISN'T my FAULT.

My mum says all the other seven-year-olds in the zoo knew what the zoo meant. Which is a lie. Because Gabby didn't understand what the zoo meant either and she's been seven for ages.

221

Dylan didn't even know! And he's as old as NINE!!!!!!!!!

Gabby and Dylan are my best friends, which is why Mum invited them to come to the zoo with me today. Going to the zoo was my special birthday treat!

The **trouble with special birthday treats** is they only happen once a year, which means they can make you a bit excited.

My mum says I hadn't got a BIT excited, I'd got OVER–OVER-excited. She says there's a big difference between being a bit excited and being over–over-excited, and that if I ever get over–over-excited like today again, then all my birthdays will be cancelled in future. Which means I'll be seven for ever.

Gabby and Dylan say that if my mum cancels all my birthdays, I can share some of theirs. Like for instance when Gabby has her next birthday, she gets half of it and I get the other half. That means, instead of Gabby being eight, she'll only go up a half to seven and a half, but I'll go up a half to seven and a half too!

Dylan says that he wants to keep three quarters of his birthday. That means on his next birthday, instead of being ten, he doesn't mind being nine and three quarters instead, which is nearly ten anyway.

Dylan says giving someone a quarter of your birthday is still quite a lot, especially when someone else has already given you one of their halves too. Plus, Dylan says if I can find another person to give me one of their quarters, then I'll be back to normal.

Except, the **trouble with me going back to normal** is it won't be right, because then I'll be going up in ones, Dylan will be going up in three quarters and Gabby will be going up in halves.

Which is less than me. Which really wouldn't be fair because I was the one that got over–over-excited at the zoo, not them.

Dylan says to make it fair, Gabby and him would need to find someone else to give them a half AND a quarter of their birthday!

BUT THAT adds up to three quarters of a birthday!!!

Dylan says that the **trouble with someone giving away three quarters of their birthday** is they'll only be getting a quarter older every year. Which really isn't very much at all.

Dylan is ever so good at maths. He's going to be a computer when he grows up.

Gabby isn't. Gabby hates adding up. And taking away. Gabby says sums make her brain shrink. The **trouble with your brain shrinking** is in the end it will turn into a pea.

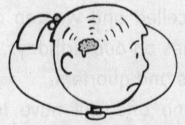

Which is the worst thing in the world a brain could turn into.

Plus your head will start to rattle.

And you won't be able to tie your shoe laces.

Or do joined up.

In the end we all agreed it would be easier if I didn't EVER get over–over-excited in zoos again. That way, what happened today will never happen again.

Plus none of my birthdays will ever get cancelled and we can all grow up in ones on our birthdays, instead of halves and quarters.

Plus no one will have to worry about blowing out more than their fair share of candles.

Or getting too many pink ones.

Gabby says just to make sure I don't get over–over-excited again, it might be better if I didn't ever go to the zoo again. EVER EVER!

Gabby said maybe we should just go swimming or something on my next birthday.

But I said no way.

Swimming pools aren't anywhere near as good as zoos. Even swimming pools with slides and wave machines and hot chocolates.

And anyway. What happened today WASN'T MY FAULT!

IT WAS THE ZOO'S FAULT!

CHAPTER 2

Do you always wake up early on your birthday? I do. Especially when I've got presents to open AND a special birthday treat with an extra-special secret surprise to find out about too!

The **trouble with special birthday treats with an extra-special secret surprise** is they make you wake up even earlier than early.

I'm not sure exactly what time it was when I woke my mum up the first time this morning. But by the third time it was 2:27.

It felt much much later than that to me. In fact it felt just like the afternoon at 2:27 this morning to me!

And at 2:49, 3:17, 3:25 and 3:33!

By 3:34 Mum's voice had gone all growly. I couldn't see her because it was too dark in the bedroom, but I recognized her growly voice.

She always does growly voices when she's grumpy.

That's the **trouble with mums at 3:34 in the morning**: they just don't care about other people's birthdays.

Mum said she did care about my birthday, but 3:34 wasn't the morning, it was the middle of the night and I should go back to bed, get under my covers, close my eyes, fall asleep and come and wake her at eight o'clock.

"Or else."

I said or else what?

She said or else I wouldn't get any birthday presents in the morning at all. I said maybe the clock in her bedroom was wrong.

She said the clock in her bedroom was never wrong. It was digital. She said digital clocks are never wrong. Especially at 3:34 in the morning. I said it was afternoon in Australia.

She said we don't live in Australia.

I said I wished we did.

She said sometimes she wished I did too.

I said, "Can't I open just one of my presents?"

She said if I didn't go back to bed RIGHT NOW, I wouldn't get any presents OR my special birthday treat OR my extra-special secret birthday surprise EITHER!

So I went back to bed.

The **trouble with going back to bed when you don't want to** is your eyelids won't close.

Well, they will close, but they won't stay closed. That's because eyelids are one of the most excited bits of your body.

I closed mine about a trillion times, but every time I thought of my presents, or wondered what my secret birthday special surprise was, they just kept pinging open again.

I even tried holding them down with my fingers, but that didn't work either. That's the **trouble with holding eyelids down with your fingers.** If your eyelids are too excited, you have to let go.

The **trouble with letting go of your eyelids when they are too excited** is your eyeballs start getting excited next.

Then your head. And then your whole body. Including your pyjamas.

If Mum had let me open just one of my presents, then I would probably have been all right. I would probably have gone straight back to sleep. My eyeballs wouldn't have got excited, my eyelids wouldn't have kept pinging open, and my whole body wouldn't have been so wriggly.

But she didn't. And they did.

That's the **trouble with not being allowed to open just ONE present**: the only thing you CAN open IS your eyes.

I didn't go to sleep at all after that.

CHAPTER 3

When my mum woke me up, it was half-past eight!

"Happy birthday, Daisy!" she said. "Wake up, Sleepy Head! It's half-past eight!!"

I told her I hadn't been asleep AT ALL, ALL NIGHT, and that it was HER FAULT because she should have let me open just ONE present.

Mum said not to worry because now I could open ALL my presents . . . !

ONCE I'd opened ALL my birthday cards.

The **trouble with being made to open your birthday cards before you've opened your presents** is birthday cards aren't anywhere near as good as presents.

Mum says that cards are important because they have birthday messages in and they tell you who the presents are from.

I got a Shaker Maker painting set from my Auntie Sue and Uncle Clive.

I got a SlippySlidy water slide that

you can squirt washing-up liquid on from my nanny and grampy, except our garden doesn't slope very much, so it won't be very slidy. It should still be quite slippy though.

Mrs Pike, my neighbour, bought me a big book on cats.

And Mum bought me a new second-hand bike! With bigger wheels and a higher saddle, plus a basket on the front to put things in, PLUS a drinks bottle full of orange squash, which is my favourite allowed drink.

But my best birthday present was my surprise birthday trip to the ZOO!

With Gabby and Dylan!

I'd known for ages I was going to have a special birthday treat, but I didn't know till this morning that I was going to be going to the ZOO!

With Dylan and Gabby too!!

Mum told me when I was eating my breakfast. I was so excited, one of my cornflakes went down sideways!

And then things got even more exciting!!!

I thought Dylan and Gabby were the extra-special secret surprise bit of my birthday treat, but I was wrong!

Dylan and Gabby coming to the zoo with me was only just one little bit of the extra-special secret surprise!

The biggest bit of my extra-special secret birthday surprise was . . .

You're never going to guess . . .

Go on, guess . . .

You'll never guess . . .

Have you guessed?

I bet you haven't.

OK, I'll tell you . . .

The biggest bit of my special secret birthday zoo surprise was . . .

I was going to FEED THE PENGUINS AT THE ZOO!

My mum had actually arranged

for me to go into the actual penguin cage with the actual zoo keeper and FEED actual penguins on my birthday! REAL ACTUAL PENGUINS! With actual beaks and everything!

How brilliant is that! Gabby and Dylan were coming to our house at 10:00, and then the three of us were going to spend a whole day at the zoo together.

Plus my mum.

PLUS, out of the WHOLE ZOO, I would be the ONLY ONE out of absolutely everyone that would be allowed to feed the actual penguins in the actual penguin cage today!

How totally totally brilliant is that!

Mum said she was pleased that I was pleased about my extra-special surprise. Then she pointed at the floor and asked if I'd like to do something extra-special for her before we got ready to go out.

That's the **trouble with birthday wrapping paper**. It always needs picking up afterwards.

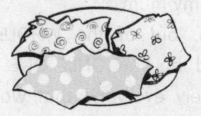

CHAPTER 4

The **trouble with waiting by the window for your best friends to turn up** is they never turn up when you want them to.

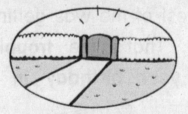

I was ready at half-past nine. Why couldn't they be too?

Mum told me to stop steaming up the glass or I'd have to clean the window with a duster.

That's the **trouble with breathing when you're excited**. Your teeth get too hot.

The rest of me was getting quite hot too. That's the **trouble with having your birthday in March**.

You have to put far more clothes on when you go out for birthday treats.

If my birthday was in the summer, I could have just worn flip-flops and shorts.

And a T-shirt.

And knickers.

And socks . . .

Actually, not socks.

Not with flip-flops anyway.

Anyway, anyway, Mum told me to take my duffle coat and scarf off and wait until Gabby and Dylan arrived before I put them on again, but I wouldn't, because I wanted to make sure I was extra-extra ready. Being extra-extra ready is really good.

When Dylan and Gabby arrived at my house, they had their coats and scarves on too.

Gabby was wearing her Wellingtons as well, just in case there was any elephant poo at the zoo.

The **trouble with treading in elephant poo** is it can go right up past your knees if you're not careful. Up to your head if you're really little!

So I put my Wellingtons on too, just in case, but Dylan didn't.

Dylan said he wasn't scared and was going in his shoes! He is nine though.

In the car on the way to the zoo, I opened my presents from Gabby and Dylan.

Gabby bought me a magic set, and Dylan gave me a rocket for letting off on the lawn plus a real actual snake skin. He said he found it in his snake tank and it came off his snake, who's called Shooter.

When I wiggled the snake skin at Gabby, she screamed and bashed it with her hand.

So it broke in half.

That's the **trouble with snake skins**: they're not meant to be bashed.

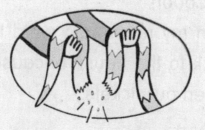

Dylan said he couldn't wait to visit the reptile house and Gabby said she was bursting to see the monkeys.

But I wanted to see the PENGUINS!

When I told Gabby and Dylan that I was actually going to feed actual penguins with actual fish out of an actual bucket, they were really jealous!

Gabby said, "Woww!" and Dylan said, "Coool!"

Then my mum said we'd have to go back to the house because she'd forgotten our tickets.

That's the **trouble with mums when they go to zoos**: they need to get more organized.

On the way back to our house, we sang Nelly the Elephant, but instead of shouting trump trump trump, we did great big elephant-poo noises! Mum let us because it was my birthday, but asked if we could sing something nicer on the way back to the zoo. No one knew any nice songs so we did animal noises instead.

The **trouble with doing animal noises** is zoo animals are really hard.

Farm animals are easy, but zoo animals aren't. No one knew what noise a rhinoceros made, or a zebra or a camel or a crocodile or even a penguin!

Gabby knew how to do monkeys and Dylan knew how to do snakes, but the only one I could think of was a lion.

Then Gabby had a brilliant idea. Why not do the sounds of a lion eating a monkey and a snake!

So we did!

Then we did the sounds of a monkey eating a snake and a lion!

But the funniest one was the sound of a snake eating a lion and a monkey!

With squirty cream!

I did the squirty-cream sound, plus the lion, and then Dylan did the sound of the snake plus some CUSTARD TOO!!

It was sooooo funny I nearly wet myself!

Mum said it was sooooo noisy too, then asked us if we would mind making the sounds of a giraffe instead.

None of us knew what a giraffe sounded like, so Mum said, "Actually, giraffes don't make any sounds at all."

Which is silly.

And impossible.

So we all made hairy gorilla noises instead.

Mum said we were getting over-excited, which wasn't true. But when we started doing dinosaur noises, she said if we didn't stop, then she would.

When we asked her what she meant, she said that if we didn't stop doing dinosaur noises right there and then, she would stop the car right there and then.

So we stopped.

And she kept going.

CHAPTER 5

When we got to the zoo, there were loads of people there already.

We had to drive for miles to find a parking space, but I didn't care. There might have been lots of people there already but I was the only one who was going to be allowed to feed the actual penguins!

The **trouble with actual penguins** is you can't just feed them when you want to.

Mum said I had to wait till feeding time, which wasn't until two o'clock!

I said they were bound to be hungry right now, and if I didn't get to feed them right away, they would probably starve to death.

Mum said they wouldn't starve to death at all and there were plenty of other animals to look at in the meantime.

Dylan wanted to go straight to the snakes, but I didn't mind where we went, and anyway the monkey house was nearest.

The **trouble with monkey houses** is they really pong. Gabby says it's the smell of you-know-what, but Dylan said it was mouldy bananas as well.

The **trouble with mouldy bananas** is they go all brown and squidgy.

My mum put one in my lunch box once, but I refused to eat it. She said it wasn't mouldy, and if I'd taken the trouble to peel it, I would have found a perfectly good banana inside.

But Gabby said if you try to peel a mouldy banana, it will explode all over your face and your school clothes, so there was no way I was going to eat it. Not even if someone tried to force me.

Monkeys don't care about exploding bananas. That's because they don't wear school clothes or even go to school.

The **trouble with going to school if you're a monkey** is you're not allowed to jump around in class.

Or swing from ropes or throw orange peel on the floor.

Jack Beechwhistle threw a crisp packet on the floor in the playground once and he got told off by the dinner lady. And he had to pick it up.

There's no way I would have invited Jack Beechwhistle to the zoo with me today.

Not unless we could have fed him to the lions.

The **trouble with lions** is they lie down too much.

At least zoo lions do. You can watch monkeys for ages because they never stop swinging around or climbing on tyres or scratching their bottoms. But lions don't have any ropes or tyres to play with. All they have is about two rocks.

They always look really puffed

out though. Except you can never tell why. Telly lions are always racing after zebras and stuff, which would definitely puff you out because zebras are really fast runners. But zoo lions never seem to do anything. Apart from twitch their tails. If you ask me, all zoo lions seem to do is lie down all the time and blink a lot.

And they've got flies on their face. Me and Gabby counted thirteen flies on one daddy lion's face.

Actually, I counted fifteen, but Gabby said I'd counted some of my flies twice.

The **trouble with counting flies on lions' faces** is the flies never stay still.

Only the lion does. One moment the flies are crawling around its eyes, the next minute they're crawling up its nose.

Gabby says lions' faces are covered in meat juice. The **trouble with meat juice** is if you don't wash it off, you get flies all over you.

Because meat juice is really attractive to flies. If lions washed their faces and paws after they'd had their zebra, they'd be all right. Trouble is, lions don't know how to use a flannel or pick up soap.

Dylan said that chameleons eat flies; so do tree frogs and so do little iguanas. So we went to the reptile house next.

CHAPTER 6

The **trouble with reptile houses** is it's really dark inside.

Gabby said it was spooky, and my mum said she couldn't see where she was going. Then Dylan said we weren't inside the reptile bit yet. We were just in the bit you have to go through first.

When we opened the next door, it got bright again, and you could see lots of different tanks made of glass. That's what reptiles live in – glass tanks instead of cages, otherwise they'll crawl through the bars and get you.

There were all sorts of different lizards in the glass tanks, and snakes and even great big frogs. They didn't do very much either, though. In fact, the snakes looked even stiller than the lions.

Gabby said it was probably because it was so hot inside. She said if she lived somewhere that was as hot as a reptile house, all she would do is lie down and eat ice creams.

Dylan said snakes don't eat ice creams and they were probably saving their energy for when they had to pounce on a locust or something else they wanted to eat. Locusts are like big grasshoppers, except they taste of Africa.

The **trouble with tasting of Africa** is that there are loads of animals that want to eat you: lions, tigers, leopards, cheetahs. But not tortoises.

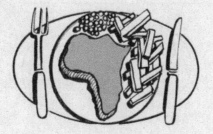

Tortoises only eat lettuce, which doesn't taste of anything. I know because I had some at my nanny and grampy's once.

The tortoises in the reptile house were being too still as well, so I tapped on their glass with my hand.

"Don't tap on the glass, Daisy," said Mum, pointing to a sign on the glass tank that said, PLEASE DO NOT TAP ON THE GLASS.

The **trouble with not tapping on the glass in the reptile house** is you'll never get anything to move.

My mum said that every time we turned round the tortoises quickly jumped up and did cartwheels behind our backs.

But each time we turned round really quickly to try and catch them out, they still looked just as still. So we went to look at some other animals.

CHAPTER 7

The **trouble with sparrows** is it's a swizz putting them in a zoo.

When we went to look at the spider monkeys, there were sparrows in the cage too! They were flying around and perching on branches and pecking at the floor and everything. Who wants to see sparrows in a zoo? You can see them in your own garden at home.

If you ask me, zoos should let all their sparrows go and put something better in the cages instead. Like budgies!

Gabby said they might be African sparrows. But they looked like normal ones to me.

The **trouble with spider monkeys** is their heads look too small.

Plus their tails look too long. Mum said that spider monkeys can use their tails just like people use their arms and legs. Their tails are really strong, which means they can hang upside down from branches and peel kiwi fruits at the same time.

I still can't see why they've got such small heads though . . .

Gabby said they probably fell from a tree when they were hanging by their tails. If you fall from a tree when you're hanging by your tail, your head will hit the ground and get banged down into your shoulders. That would definitely make your head look really small.

Dylan said they were just weird.

Not as weird as a fossa though. Me, Gabby and Dylan had never heard of a fossa before. Even my mum hadn't heard of a fossa, and she's heard of everything! But fossas do exist because we nearly actually saw one. And boy, do they look weird!

They've got the whiskers of an otter, the nose of a dog, the tail of a cat and the smooth brown body of an ottercatdog!! How weird is that?

The **trouble with fossas** is they hide a lot, which means that if you look through the glass, you don't actually get to see an actual fossa.

You can see the actual picture of them on the cage, though.

Mum said that fossas are like ugly tree lions, and they can chase through trees just like a squirrel. Except they don't chase nuts. They chase lemurs!

To eat!

Gabby reckons fossas eat cars, too, because there were two dead tyres on the floor of the fossa's cage. All the rest of the car had been eaten! Dylan said there was no way that any animal could eat a car. Except for a tyrannosaurus rex. But me and Gabby definitely reckoned the fossa tyres had been chewed.

Then we looked for bits of dead lemur. But we couldn't see any. So we went to look at the alive ones.

The **trouble with alive lemurs** is they look like spider monkeys.

Plus they haven't got any thumbs. Not proper thumbs like proper humans anyway. Mum said that they'd be no good at hitchhiking. But we didn't know what she meant. Then she said that considering they didn't have proper thumbs, they were really good at peeling oranges.

There were dead bits of actual fruit all over the lemurs' floor.

The **trouble with dead bits of actual fruit** is they make the cage look really untidy.

Mum said the floor of the lemur cage reminded her of the floor in my bedroom. Which is a lie, because the only fruit I've ever left on my carpet is about three apple cores.

And a banana skin.

But not a mouldy one. And not all at the same time either. Like a lemur would.

Plus I don't like kiwi fruit. It's got too many pips.

The **trouble with pips** is they don't taste very nice.

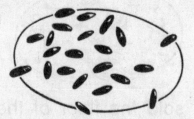

If you had lemur teeth, they'd probably taste all right, but if you've got normal teeth, then they don't taste very nice at all. Especially if you crunch one.

My mum bought a big bunch of grapes from the supermarket once and they were full of pips. In fact, there were more pips than grape! She said she'd meant to buy pipless grapes, but the supermarket was closing so she'd just grabbed the nearest ones.

The **trouble with just grabbing the nearest ones** is you can end up spitting pips out for ages.

Mum only buys pipless grapes now. But mostly she buys apples.

Or bananas. And tangerines at Christmas. But not kiwis.

Because of the pips.

CHAPTER 8

After the lemurs we went to see the llamas.

The **trouble with llamas** is they might spit at you even if they're not eating grapes!

My mum says llamas only spit at people when they're frightened, and the thing to do is watch their ears. If the ears of a llama go back, then it means they're going to spit and you should run away as fast as you can.

Gabby reckons llamas only spit at people who call them names. They'd probably spit at Jack Beechwhistle then, 'cos he's always calling people names.

I bet if he saw a llama, he'd call it Goofy or something, just because its teeth stick out and look all funny. Jack Beechwhistle called Melanie Beamish "Bugs Bunny" once at school, and her teeth hardly stick out at all. She didn't spit at him, though. We're not allowed to do spits at school. She whacked him on the back with her lunch box instead.

Dylan says animal teeth have different designs, depending on what sort of food they eat. Lions have biting teeth, hyenas have crunching teeth, giraffes have munching teeth and humming birds have sucking teeth. Which you can't actually see because they're so small.

Elephants have the biggest teeth. Did you know an elephant's tooth is the size of a brick and weighs three kilos! That's heavier than a flower pot! It's definitely true because it said so on the sign on the wall outside the elephant cage.

Imagine being a tooth fairy and having to pick up an elephant's tooth! Gabby reckons it would take about twenty tooth fairies all at once to pick up an elephant's tooth. I reckon tooth fairies have special fairy cranes for doing really heavy zoo jobs.

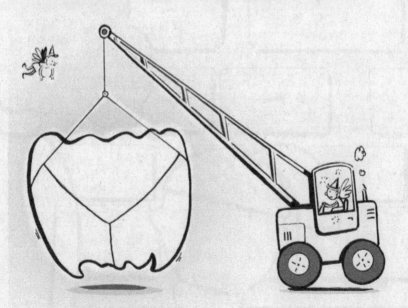

There were loads of signs on the walls at the zoo. At first I didn't take much notice of them because the animals were too exciting, but when we went to see the sea lions, the whole wall was covered in signs!

Mum said they weren't signs, they were plaques, and each plaque meant that someone had adopted a sea lion. She said that zoos liked visitors to adopt their animals because it helped the zoo to look after them.

Loads of people had adopted the sea lions. I reckon it's because they've got really cute faces.

And they're really good swimmers. Mum said that sea lions have special nostrils that close tightly when they put their whiskers under the water. Sea-lion nostrils are so good they can stay under water for forty minutes! So can the rest of the sea lion!!

I tried holding my breath underwater in the bath once, but I could only do it for about one second. Plus the water went up my nose. That's because I haven't got sea-lion nostrils. Or a snorkel.

The **trouble with snorkels** is my mum won't let me have one.

Or a deep-sea diving suit. I saw a deep-sea diver on the telly once and it was really good.

If you've got a deep-sea diving suit, you get to do lots of roly-polys backwards off of boats. And you get to swim with actual sharks.

The **trouble with actual sharks** is they'd be better if they only had sucking teeth.

If sharks had sucking teeth like a humming bird instead of biting teeth like a lion, then they wouldn't look so scary. Plus they wouldn't be able to chomp you, they'd only be able to suck you.

Whales only suck, and they don't look scary at all. Even great big whales don't look scary. They always look gentle and kind.

The **trouble with trying to fit a whale in a zoo** is there wouldn't be any space for any other animals.

Apart from leaf-cutter ants. That's why you never see whales in zoos.

CHAPTER 9

About the biggest thing you can fit in a zoo is an elephant. Then it's a rhinoceros.

The **trouble with rhinoceroses** is they should go to the loo before the zoo opens.

Gabby, Dylan and me were looking down over the wall into the great big space where they lived, when the rhino did the most ginormous disgusting wee! It was so ginormous and so disgusting that we had to close our eyes.

We closed our eyes and counted to ten, but when we opened them again, it was still doing it!

Dylan reckoned it did enough wee to fill two paddling pools! I reckon rhinos should be banned if they're going to do things like that in front of children on their birthday.

Mum said that when you're a rhino, you can just do what you want when you want. Because no one's going to stop you.

The **trouble with trying to stop a rhino** is they're made out of concrete.

If you try and stop a rhino doing a wee or anything, it will run you over and squash you flat or bash you up into the air with its horn.

Dylan said a rhino's horn isn't made out of concrete, it's made out of hair. Special hairy concrete-type hair that you only get in Africa.

Anyway, even if a rhino horn really is only made out of hair, it can still give you a really hard bash.

The other **trouble with white rhinos** is they're not that white.

The sign said it was a "White Rhino", but the one at our zoo was brown.

Gabby said it wasn't brown, it was mud, and it was probably white underneath the brown mud. I said it should stop getting so muddy or everyone would think it was a liar, but Dylan said it needed the mud for camouflage.

The **trouble with camouflage** is it makes things really hard to see.

Apart from the Nile monitor lizard. I saw him straight away.

Camouflage is like wearing special clothes that make you invisible. Lizards' camouflage is the colour of leaves, butterflies' camouflage is the colour of flower petals, zebras' camouflage is the colour of stripy grass and the Loch Ness monster's camouflage is the colour of Loch Ness.

That's why no one's ever seen it. Including deep-sea divers.

The worst kind of zoo camouflage is the flamingos. They're easy peasy to see, because flamingos aren't the same colour as anything. They're just pink. Bright pink, too! And they stand on one leg.

The **trouble with standing on one leg when you're pink** is it makes you look like a stick of candyfloss.

Dylan says if animals don't taste nice, sometimes they have really bright colours on them to warn other animals not to bite them.

I said that if I was going to warn an animal not to bite me, I'd make myself look like a pea, not something as yummy as candyfloss.

Then Mum said we should all try standing on one leg too. Dylan did it

for the longest, then me, then Gabby,
except Gabby said I pushed her but
I didn't. I just sort of fell on her, but I
couldn't help it.

Mum read the sign on the flamingo fence and told us that a flamingo can stand on one leg for up to four hours without putting its foot down. Or even wobbling!

Trouble is, we didn't really have long enough to see if it was true, because straight after the flamingos it was time for my birthday zoo lunch!

CHAPTER 10

I love birthday zoo lunches!

Last year, I had a birthday Wacky Playpark lunch, but birthday zoo lunches are even better!

After we had found a bench to sit on that was sort of out of the wind, Mum took our birthday zoo sandwiches out of her bag. Most of the time in my sandwiches I only get to have cheese or jam. But when it's my birthday, my mum lets me have whatever I want!

"WITHIN REASON."

Because birthday sandwiches are really special!

Dylan said he had Bully Bear in his sandwiches at school but he'd never had it with hundreds and thousands on.

Gabby said Bully Bear with hundreds and thousands on tasted really nice and she was going to try hundreds and thousands with cheese spread when she got home.

The **trouble with trying hundreds and thousands with cheese spread** is you'd better ask your mum first.

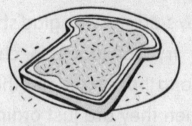

Because it needs to be your
birthday really. Otherwise your mum
will probably say, "No, you can't have
hundreds and thousands on your
cheese spread. Are you mad? Put
the hundreds and thousands back in
the cupboard right now."

I was nearly going to have
special birthday mini sausages
dipped in chocolate spread too. But I
tried them at home, and they weren't
very nice. So I didn't.

Gabby said she was glad she didn't have to try sausages in chocolate spread, and that sometimes things are nicer when they are just ordinary.

That's why we had ordinary sausages and cheesy puffs not dipped in anything. And we had chicken saté sticks AND we had lemonade (which is my favourite not-allowed drink)!

While we were sitting on the bench eating our lunch, loads of birds started coming all around us. There were sparrows that had escaped out of their cages, plus about seven pigeons, three ducks and a yellow tit. Except Mum said it was a greenfinch.

Except it didn't look very green to me.

Dylan said that in the winter, birds find it really hard to find food. That's why people hang peanuts up in their gardens.

Gabby said the birds had definitely smelled our Bully Bear with hundreds and thousands on, and we had better eat our sandwiches fast!

The **trouble with eating your sandwiches fast** is if you're not careful, you might choke.

I was really careful because I didn't want to drop any of my hundreds and thousands, but Gabby wasn't careful at all.

So she ended up choking all over the place. And scaring the birds.

AND she had to borrow some of my lemonade to wash her sandwich down. Which wasn't fair because she'd already had her own lemonade. Plus I like lemonade more than she does.

And it was my birthday, not hers.

Which means I should have got the most lemonade out of everyone.

But I didn't.

Because of Gabby's chokes.

Which isn't fair. But it ended up all right. Because Mum said I could have some more lemonade when we got home.

After Gabby had stopped choking, we had chocolate mini rolls.

The **trouble with chocolate mini rolls** is they're not as big as a proper birthday cake.

They do taste really nice, though! Mum said Nanny and Grampy were coming to see me when we got back from the zoo and Nanny was going to bring a special zoo birthday cake that she had baked all by herself, with an apron and everything!

Gabby said it was probably a good idea to have my big cake later, because if elephants sniffed a big cake, it would make them stampede all over us.

Stampedes are when loads of animals break out of their cages and run at you to get your cake.

Dylan said he saw a stampede of cows in a film once and they ran over everything, including bushes, fences and a river. Plus they flattened a cowboy.

He was probably the one holding the cake.

I wonder if it was his birthday too?

CHAPTER 11

The **trouble with putting birthday candles on a chocolate mini roll** is it's really hard to fit seven candles on.

Even five is hard. Plus when you stick the candles in, the chocolate on the outside starts to break off.

Mum said I might have to settle for one candle instead of seven, but I said I wanted seven candles –

otherwise people might think I was one, which is a baby.

The **trouble with trying to light seven candles on a mini roll after you've managed to fit them on** is the wind keeps blowing them out before you get a chance to blow.

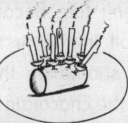

Or even huff.

Or sing "Happy Birthday".

Which is really a nuisance.

Plus the candles go wonky.

Then the chocolate starts to melt.

Then the mini roll goes sticky.

Which is all right if you're the one who's holding it, because then you get to lick the chocolate off your fingers. But if your mum is holding it, then she gets to lick her fingers instead.

Which isn't fair, because it's not her mini roll in the first place. It's mine. So I should be the one that gets to lick the chocolate off.

Mum said if I didn't stop moaning about melted chocolate, she would feed all our mini rolls to the monkeys!

Which was a lie. Because if she

did, there would be a stampede. Which would be her fault, not mine.

Then she'd get into trouble, not me.

And anyway, the wind suddenly stopped blowing.

"QUICK, QUICK, QUICK!" said Mum. "BLOW, BLOW, BLOW!"

So I did!

After I'd blown out my candles, Mum, Gabby and Dylan sang "Happy Birthday", and then Mum gave them each a mini roll too.

But not with candles. Because it wasn't their birthday.

Plus theirs weren't sticky.

When I asked my mum if I could have one that wasn't sticky as well, she said one mini roll was enough, and if I ate too many mini rolls, the zoo keeper would think I was an elephant.

Which isn't true either. Because I haven't got a trunk.

Or massive teeth.

Anyway, there weren't any more mini rolls left.

So we had apples.

The **trouble with apples** is I had one with a maggot in once.

It came off a tree in my nanny and grampy's garden. Luckily I didn't bite through the maggot, I only bit through its hole. But it still wasn't very nice.

I do still like apples because they're juicy, but I always double-check for maggot holes before I eat one now.

Especially if I'm at my nanny and grampy's house.

When we'd finished our apples, Mum looked at her watch and then put all our rubbish into a bag.

"I think we should make our way over in the direction of the penguins, don't you, Daisy?" smiled Mum.

"Yes, yes, yes, yes, yes!" said me!

CHAPTER 12

The **trouble with zoo bins** is sometimes they get really full. We had to really squeeze our apple cores in to stop them falling back out onto the ground.

But then Gabby's fell out again.

And then Dylan's fell out when Gabby put hers back in.

So in the end Mum put all our

apple cores back in the bag, and said she would take our rubbish home.

After we'd visited the litter bin, we went to look at the meerkats.

The **trouble with meerkats** is, WATCH OUT IF YOU'RE A SCORPION OR A SNAKE!

Because if a meerkat catches you, it will gobble you up!

Lots of people had adopted the meerkats. That's because meerkats are really good.

"ZEETU" HAS BEEN ADOPTED BY IVYDALE PRIMARY SCHOOL.
RANI HAS ADOPTED "CARLTON" 2007
2007 WHISKERS HAS BEEN ADOPTED BY ANGEL
2008 BENISHA HAS ADOPTED "SCRUFF"
"CARLOS" HAS BEEN ADOPTED 2005.
"STARSKY" ADOPTED BY ALAN BARR AGED 9
2003 "KENDI" HAS BEEN ADOPTED BY KATIE ADAMS
2001
"MAC
"HUTCH
"WILSON
"ZAPPA"
"BINA" HAS BEEN ADOPTED BY MR + MRS NEECH
"POINTER"

It said on the sign next to the adopting plaques that meerkats are immune to deadly poison! That means that even if a snake bites and bites and bites them or a scorpion stings and stings and stings them, the meerkat will just eat the snake or scorpion anyway. Without being poisoned or even getting a tummy-ache!

Dylan said he wouldn't let a meerkat anywhere near the snake tank in his bedroom.

And Gabby wondered whether meerkats could eat swede without dying too.

The next sign we saw was for the pygmy goats. The **trouble with pygmy goats** is their poos look like currants, which could be really dangerous if you were making cakes in the zoo.

Dylan said he didn't think zoos made cakes, in case of the stampedes, so we were probably safe, but Gabby said that in future if she ever went into a zoo shop to buy something to eat, she would never buy a currant cake in case it had a pygmy-goat poo in it. In fact, just to be totally safe she was going to totally stick to ice creams.

The **trouble with ice creams** is it's really hard to get your mum to buy you one when it's March.

Especially if you've already had mini rolls and lemonade. Mum said it was too cold for ice creams, and anyway we'd all had a birthday zoo lunch.

The **trouble with birthday zoo lunches** is they really make you need an ice cream. Especially MY birthday zoo lunches.

It took me about ten minutes to persuade Mum that we all really really really needed ice creams. At first she wouldn't listen, but in the end she did a big sigh and she said we just had time to go to buy some, before we went to the penguins.

The **trouble with ice-cream cabinets in zoo shops on March 3rd** is there aren't any ice creams in them.

There isn't anything in them at all! Apart from cold air.

The lady behind the counter said ice creams were out of season and they wouldn't be getting any in until Easter.

So we had to have sweets instead.

The **trouble with sweets** is you're not allowed to feed them to the animals.

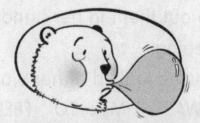

I saw some white-nosed coatis who really looked like they wanted a Tic-Tac, but Mum said all the animals in the zoo were on carefully controlled diets that didn't include Tic-Tacs, Refreshers or Hubba Bubba bubble gum.

I said if they liked fruit, they were bound to like strawberry

Hubba Bubba, but Mum gave me one of her looks and said if we couldn't control our sweets, then we would have to put them in her handbag for safekeeping.

Then she looked at her watch.

IT WAS TIME TO FEED THE PENGUINS!

CHAPTER 13

My heart was beating really fast when we arrived at the penguin house. Mum said hers was too, but that was because she isn't used to running.

When we got there, a zoo man in a brown uniform with a zoo badge on it was waiting for us by the gate.

"Are you Daisy?" he asked.

"Yes!" said my mum, pointing to me. "Sorry we're late!"

"That's fine," said the zoo man. "My name's Tim. Happy birthday,

Daisy! Would you like to feed the penguins?"

"YES, PLEASE!" I said.

"Then come with me," said Tim, "and I'll introduce you to Tiffany."

I thought Tiffany was going to be the penguin leader. But she wasn't. She was a zoo lady. Tiffany had a brown uniform with a zoo badge too, plus she was wearing Wellingtons. That's because everyone who's an expert on penguins wears Wellingtons.

Mum asked me if I wanted her to come with me, but I said no because she wasn't wearing Wellingtons.

The **trouble with not wearing Wellingtons** is penguins won't really like you.

So I told Mum it would probably be better if she went to sit with Gabby and Dylan. You can still watch penguins being fed if you haven't got Wellingtons, and they will still like you a bit. But not as much, because they're only liking you through the glass.

Mum took Gabby and Dylan into the bit behind the glass where they could sit and watch me and the penguins, and then Tiffany held my hand.

Then my heart started beating EVEN FASTER because I was actually going in!

Right in!! Into the penguin house. With the actual penguins!!!!!!!

First of all we went down a slope, then up a bit to a gate that had two padlocks and two bolts on it. Tiffany undid the padlocks and then opened the gate. I couldn't see any penguins at first because

Tiffany's zoo shirt was in the way. But when we walked right inside through the gate, there were penguins all over the place!

Plus there was a baby penguin too!

CHAPTER 14

The **trouble with baby penguins** is they can't really do very much. Except sort of stand still.

Tiffany said that baby penguins don't get their proper feathers until they are about six months old, which means they can't swim around like their mummies and daddies can.

Mummy and daddy penguins

have special swimming feathers that keep water out and stop them getting soggy. Baby penguins don't have proper feathers at all. All baby penguins have is fluff.

Which doesn't keep water out.

But it does make them look reeeeaaaaallly cute.

Tiffany knew loads about penguins. When she was opening the penguin cupboard, she said there were eighteen different types of penguin in the world. Not including the chocolate biscuit ones.

The ones we were going to feed were called Humboldt penguins.

Which isn't a very good name for a
type of penguin, I think.

Plus it's really hard to spell.

Anyway, when the mummy and
daddy penguins saw Tiffany open

the cupboard, they started jumping off the rocks and diving into the pool. Then they started zooming through the water and doing sort of sideways roly-polys.

Tiffany said they looked really hungry, and then she asked me if I was any good at throwing fish.

I said I was really good, which was a bit of a fib because I'd never thrown a fish before. I'd thrown tennis balls and frisbees in the park, and I threw a stone at school once, but I got told off for doing that.

Anyway, I just knew I'd be really good at throwing fish.

Then I saw Mum through the glass on the other side of the pool! And Gabby and Dylan! They were sitting in the middle of a huge crowd of people and they were waving.

I waved back, and then my mum got her camera out to take a picture.

The **trouble with saying "cheese" when you're about to feed the penguins** is you can't really.

Otherwise the penguins might think you're going to feed them cheese and not fish. Penguins don't like cheese. It's not fishy enough.

The only thing that's fishy enough for penguins is actual fish.

The **trouble with saying "fish" when you're having your photo taken** is it makes your lips look funny. Which spoils the picture.

So I didn't say anything. I just smiled at my mum's camera instead. And waved.

Then Tiffany brought me a bucket! Not a red plastic bucket like our one at home, but a proper zoo bucket made especially for penguins out of real metal.

"Here you go, Daisy!" said Tiffany. "Make sure they all get their fair share!"

Then I looked inside the bucket.

Well, you should have seen how many fish there were inside! There were dead fish right up to the top!

CHAPTER 15

At first I thought they were alive fish in the bucket, but they weren't. They were all dead and silver with red eyes. That's just how penguins like them.

When I picked the first fish up, it felt a bit cold and slippery. I only picked it up by its tail. Just in case it WAS still alive. Plus I didn't know what it would feel like.

The **trouble with dead fish** is they feel a bit strange at first. Even if you only pick them up by the tail.

The **trouble with picking a dead fish up by the tail** is it makes it quite hard to throw.

My first fish didn't go anywhere near where I meant it to, but a penguin still got it anyway. In fact, THREE penguins zoomed right after it but only one managed to get it.

Everyone in the crowd cheered when the fish got gobbled! So next time I threw two fish at once!!

You should have seen the penguins then! I never knew they could swim so fast. The fish were only in the water for about a second before both of them had been gobbled up!!

Then I threw three fish at once, and they got gobbled up really quickly too!!!

After about five throws I was putting my fingers right into the bucket, right round the dead fish and everything. Without them feeling cold or slippery at all!

I'd really got the hang of throwing, and I was making the penguins zoom absolutely everywhere!

The penguins must have been REALLY hungry because the more I threw, the more they dived and zoomed.

One penguin even got out of the pool to try and steal a fish OUT OF MY BUCKET!

Everyone laughed, and Tiffany had to shoo him straight back into the pool.

It was soooooooo brilliant! Everyone was cheering and clapping, and there were bubbles coming out of the water, and splashes, and really fast beaks zooming everywhere.

Plus I was a really good thrower. Just like I said I would be.

When I did my second-best throw, it went right across into the corner of the penguin pool. But my BEST throw was SOOOO good, it went right over the pool, through the air and hit the glass on the other side, where Mum,

Gabby and Dylan were sitting. Everyone really laughed and clapped then!

Gabby and Dylan thought it was hilarious!

My mum tried to take a picture. But she missed it.

That's the **trouble with mums taking good pictures**. They're a bit slow.

So then I tried to throw a fish right out of the zoo! But I only had three fish left in my bucket, and they were really slippery ones. Plus one didn't have a head. So they only went as far as the middle.

But Mum still took a picture. And everyone still clapped! And the penguins kept diving and zooming around.

Then my bucket ran out.

The **trouble with buckets running out** is you don't have any fish left to throw.

Which isn't very good, because the penguins still looked really hungry.

So I threw the bucket into the penguin pool too.

I didn't actually mean to throw the bucket in – it just sort of came out of my hands. I wasn't trying to throw it in on purpose or anything. I just thought there might be some fish juice left in the bottom and the penguins might like to lick it out.

Penguins love fish juice.

The **trouble with zoo buckets** is that they sink. Because they're metal.

Plus if they land on a penguin, they can give it a really big bump on the head.

Luckily all the penguins dived out of the way, but the zoo bucket sank right to the bottom of the water.

At first everyone laughed and cheered. Except my mum. Mum covered her eyes and went red, but most people thought it was funny. Gabby and Dylan thought it was hilaaaaaaaaaaaaaaaaaaarious!

I'm not sure if Tiffany did, though. She sort of smiled and sort of frowned at the same time. And then she had to go and get a long zoo net.

The **trouble with zoo nets** is they're not very good at picking up buckets.

Which meant Tiffany had to spend quite a long time trying to get the bucket out. I asked her if she wanted me to have a go, but she said it would be better if I left it to her.

So I did.

It would definitely have been better if she had let me have a go with the net, because I'm really expert at that too.

In Cornwall when I was on holiday, Mum bought me a net. When I put it in the rock pool, I caught loads of sand, two shells and a lolly stick on my very first go! I nearly caught some weed too, but it escaped when I lifted the net up.

Tiffany took loads of goes before she even caught anything.

By the time she'd put the bucket back in the penguin cupboard and taken me back to Mum, Dylan and Gabby, most of the people behind the glass had gone. Mum said the elephants were being fed at 2:30 and everyone had probably gone to see them.

Plus she said sorry to Tiffany.

Tiffany said it was OK and she hoped I'd had a good time.

I said I'd had a REALLY good time.

Tiffany said I was SO good at throwing fish I'd be after her job one day. Then she asked me if I would like her job one day?

I said yes, but actually I fibbed, because I wouldn't want to do a job with a brown shirt. I wouldn't mind the badge though.

Except I think I'd want a growling lion on my badge. Not a paw print.

Then we waved goodbye to the penguins.

CHAPTER 16

On the way back from the penguin house, Gabby couldn't stop giggling. Dylan thought it was really funny too.

"What if you'd hit a penguin on the head?" laughed Dylan.

"What if a penguin had thought the bucket was a fish? And swallowed it!" laughed Gabby.

That's the **trouble with Gabby**.

She might have had Wellingtons on, but she's not the slightest bit expert about penguins.

Then Mum asked us where we'd like to go next.

So I said, "Home."

"HOME?" said Mum. "Surely you don't want to go home yet! We haven't seen the crocodiles, or the tigers or the vultures or the mongooses."

So I told her I was really tired.

"You're not worried about the bucket are you, Daisy?" she said. "You really shouldn't be worried about the bucket."

So I told her that the **trouble with doing really good throws** is it can really make your arms ache, and that I REALLY wanted to go home.

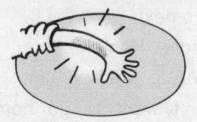

"REALLY?" she said.

"REALLY, REALLY," I said.

"But we haven't even seen the giraffes yet!" said Mum. "We must go and see the giraffes!"

"Yes, we have seen the giraffes," I said. "They were over on the other side of the rhinoceros bit."

"Well, we haven't seen the giraffes close up," said Mum.

My mum really likes giraffes.

I said we didn't need to see a giraffe close up, because they're so tall. You can see a giraffe from anywhere.

So Mum sighed, and then asked Gabby and Dylan what they wanted to do.

Gabby said she wanted to go to the play area and Dylan said, "Are there any rhinoceros beetles?"

Which was a real nuisance, because I really wanted to go home.

Mum said if there were any

rhinoceros beetles, they were probably in the reptile house. But Dylan said rhinoceros beetles weren't reptiles, they were insects. Dylan said rhinoceros beetles are the strongest animals in the world and they can lift things that are 850 times heavier than themselves. Which IS quite cool, but I REALLY REALLY wanted to go home.

Luckily the zoo didn't have any rhinoceros beetles. They did have hissing cockroaches, but Dylan said they wouldn't be as good.

The **trouble with play areas** is the zoo DID have one of them.

When we got there, it had slides and rope bridges and tunnels and everything. Gabby and Dylan couldn't wait to go on them, but I REALLY REALLY wanted to go home.

So I sat on a bench with my mum.

"Are you sure you're feeling all right, Daisy?" asked Mum. "You love swings and slides usually. I can never get you OFF the swings and slides when we go to the park!"

I said I was feeling fine, but I REALLY REALLY REALLY wanted to go home.

Luckily there was a puddle at the bottom of the big slide.

The **trouble with big slides** is they make you come down so fast, you can't stop yourself at the bottom.

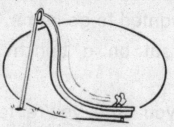

So if there's a puddle at the bottom, your bottom goes straight in it.

Gabby came down first.

And then Dylan.

You should have seen Gabby's
face. She had dirty puddle water
all over her coat and all down her
tights.

Dylan didn't get so much on him, because Gabby's bottom had already soaked a lot of the puddle up, but he still made his jeans really dirty.

Mum brushed Dylan and Gabby's bottoms down with her glove and then said that actually, it probably WAS time to go home.

Which made me really pleased.

"Have you had a good time?!" asked Mum. "Apart from the muddy bottoms!"

"YEEEESSSSSS!!!" we shouted.

"Have you had a lovely birthday, Daisy?" she asked.

"You bet!" I said.

"Come on, then," said Mum. "Let's make our way back to the car."

CHAPTER 17

The **trouble with making your way back to a car** is you can never remember where you parked it.

Mum said she was sure our car was somewhere over somewhere, but when we got somewhere over somewhere, it wasn't there at all. There were so many lines of cars everywhere, we couldn't see our car anywhere.

First we walked down one row, then we walked down another row, then we thought we'd found our car, but it was someone else's, then we walked down about a hundred more rows, then we ended up back where we started, then we didn't know where we were.

In the end we did find our car, but it wasn't somewhere over somewhere, it was somewhere over somewhere totally else.

Mum said that next time she parked a car at the zoo, she was going to ask a giraffe to stand beside it.

And just to make extra sure, she was going to ask the giraffe to wave a big flag.

On the way home Dylan and Gabby wanted to do animal noises again. Gabby said she'd found out what sound a sea lion made, and Dylan said he'd learned how to do a macaw.

But I said I didn't want to play. I said I just wanted to go home.

Gabby said, "Let's sing Nelly the Elephant again", but I said I didn't want to do that either.

Mum said I must be coming down with something, and she'd "dose me up" when we got home.

I said I didn't want any medicine and I just really really needed to get home.

We were NEARLY almost totally home too, when it happened.

CHAPTER 18

"Mu-uuuum," I said, just as we'd turned off the roundabout near our house. "Do you think we could stop off at the shops?"

"What for, Daisy?" said Mum. "You've already had lemonade and sweets today."

So I said, "I need to buy a bag of frozen peas."

Now the **trouble with saying "I need to buy a bag of frozen peas"** **when your mum knows you really really don't like peas** is that your mum will get very suspicious.

"What on earth do you want with a bag of frozen peas!!?" asked Mum.

"I need it to keep my baby penguin cold," said me.

The **trouble with mums putting their foot down on a car brake really hard** is it makes everyone shoot forward really fast and it makes you think you're going to crash.

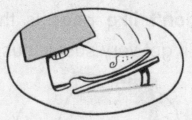

Luckily we all had our seatbelts on, but it was still really really scary and our tyres did the really realliest loudest screech ever.

"I've called him Findus," I said.

The **trouble with having a baby penguin under your duffelcoat** is, well, lots of things really.

"WHAT ARE YOU DOING WITH A PENGUIN UNDER YOUR DUFFEL COAT!"

screamed Mum, staring down at my lap with her mouth really really wide open.

"I've adopted him," I said.

"ADOPTED HIM!" squealed Mum. "YOU CAN'T ADOPT AN ANIMAL FROM THE ZOO!"

"Everyone else has," I said.

Then Gabby and Dylan undid their seatbelts really quickly and dived over my shoulders to have a look.

"WOW!" said Gabby.

"COOL!" said Dylan.

"Oh my God, we're going to prison," said my mum. "We've kidnapped a penguin and WE'RE GOING TO PRISON!"

"Can I stroke him?" said Gabby.

"Can I stroke him next?" said Dylan.

"When did you kidnap a penguin?"

said Mum. "HOW did you kidnap a penguin?"

"When Tiffany was getting the bucket out with the net," I said. "All the mummy and daddy penguins were zooming after the net and they'd left the baby one all alone. Tiffany wasn't looking after him, and the mummy and daddy penguins weren't looking after him, so I decided I would. And anyway, I haven't kidnapped him, I've adopted him."

"DAISY, DAISY, DAISY!" said Mum. "When people adopt animals at the zoo, they don't take them home with them! They just give the zoo some money to help look after them. Looking after animals is a very expensive business and adopting an animal is just a kind and helpful way of making sure all the zoo animals are well cared for.

"NO ONE TAKES ADOPTED ANIMALS HOME!"

"Christopher Dowsett is adopted," I said. "And he lives at home."

"Christopher Dowsett isn't a zoo animal, Daisy," said Mum. "He's one of your friends at school!"

"He's still adopted," I said.

"Yes, Daisy," said Mum. "Christopher

is still adopted, but when zoos say 'adopt an animal', they don't mean adopt an animal like they mean adopt a Christopher Dowsett! They mean a different kind of adopted."

"Then they shouldn't say 'adopt an animal'," I said.

"They should say 'pay for an animal' instead.

"Or 'buy food for an animal'."

"And straw," said Gabby.

"And heat pads," said Dylan.

"Well, whatever they should say, we're taking him **STRAIGHT BACK!**" said Mum.

The **trouble with penguin beaks** is they can't speak.

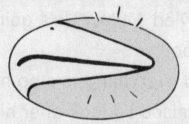

If Findus could have talked, he would definitely have told Mum that he really really didn't want to go back to the zoo and he much preferred being with me.

"But he's all fluffy, and he's all snuggled up and his wings are all flat and nice to stroke, which means he really likes me!" I said.

"Can I have a feel?" said Gabby.

"Can I have a stroke?" said Dylan.

"I don't care how fluffy and nice he is," growled Mum. "He's going back to the zoo!"

I tried everything to stop her.

I promised I'd look after him.

I promised I'd put him in my front basket and take him for rides on my new bike.

I promised I'd get a job to pay for his fish.

I promised I'd let him sleep with me. And have baths with me, in water that wasn't too hot.

I even promised I'd take him to school with me so that he could learn how to read and write and skip and everything.

I bet none of the penguins at the zoo know how to read and write. Or skip.

But Mum still made me take Findus back.

That's **the trouble with mums whose children have adopted baby penguins**: they're just not fair!

CHAPTER 19

When we got back to the zoo, the zoo was on amber alert. If a lion or a rhinoceros had been missing, then it would have been a red alert, but as it was only a baby penguin, it was just an amber one.

My mum's face was on red alert though when she gave Findus back. She said it was ever so embarrassing, and she was ever so EVER SO sorry, and I hadn't meant any harm, and I'd just misunderstood what 'adopt an animal' meant.

WHICH ISN'T MY FAULT!

The zoo were OK about it. They said they were just pleased to have Findus back. In fact, I'm not really sure what all the fuss was about.

After we'd dropped Gabby and Dylan off, Mum's face went all kind of strange and funny looking.

Then she started talking to herself.

"Out of all the mums in all the world, guess WHOSE daughter kidnaps a penguin from the zoo?" she said.

I decided I wouldn't say anything for a while; at least until we'd got

back into the house and she'd had a
cup of tea.

Trouble is, her face still looked
kind of strange and funny, even after
a cup of tea.

And after three crunchy creams!

So I decided I'd go upstairs to my bedroom and play with my birthday presents for a while.

The **trouble with birthday presents** is they're not as good as baby penguins.

Even magic sets with actual wands aren't as good as baby penguins.

So I wasn't really in the right mood to play with my birthday presents.

After about an hour, I went back

downstairs to see if Mum's face had got any better.

It hadn't. It had got worse.

"DAISY!" she growled. "DON'T YOU EVER STEAL A BABY PENGUIN FROM THE ZOO AGAIN!" she said. "IT'S A GOOD JOB IT'S YOUR BIRTHDAY," she said, "OR . . . OR . . . WELL, I DON'T KNOW WHAT I'D HAVE DONE."

Then her face went even stranger and funnier. Plus growlier.

"PROMISE ME, DAISY!" she said. "PROMISE ME YOU WILL NEVER STEAL A BABY PENGUIN FROM A ZOO AGAIN . . . OR A BABY CROCODILE OR A BABY ELEPHANT OR A BABY ANYTHING!"

So I promised.

I was going to double promise, but before I could say the words, our front doorbell rang.

Nanny and Grampy had arrived, with my special home-made birthday zoo cake!

CHAPTER 20

The **trouble with special home-made birthday zoo cakes** is sometimes the penguins on the icing look like zebras.

Especially if the person who's done them is really old. Nanny said she'd done all the penguins on the icing without copying, but apart from them being black and white, they still looked like zebras to me.

The candles looked like candles though, and I had a really good time blowing out seven more all over again!

Then everyone sang "Happy Birthday" AGAIN!

And then Nanny and Grampy gave me ANOTHER present!

Nanny said it was only something small for my new bike, but it was BRILLIANT! A real hooter that makes real loud hooting noises when you squeeze it!

Mum said it would be like living with a sea lion.

Grampy said he would fix it to my handlebars before they went home, and then he asked me to tell him all about the penguins I had fed at the zoo today.

When I looked at Mum, her face had gone a bit funny again, but then she put her finger to her lips and smiled.

So I told Nanny and Grampy about
all the penguins I'd met.
(Except one.
One little one.)

Then I told them about the
rhinoceros,

the lions,

the meerkats,

the flamingos,

the pygmy goats

and all the other
animals I could
remember,

 including the
fossa!

And guess what? Nanny and Grampy hadn't heard of a fossa either!

They hadn't heard of loads of the things that I learned at the zoo today!

Before they left, Nanny and Grampy gave me seven birthday kisses goodbye, EACH!!

Then Mum let me have seven extra hoots on my hooter and asked me to have my bath and get ready for bed.

Before she tucked me up, she read me a story (I wanted seven, but she said no), then she stroked

my forehead and asked me to promise her again that I would NEVER adopt a zoo animal again without asking her first.

So this time I double promised.

In fact I triple promised.

But that's the **trouble with double and triple promising after you've adopted a baby penguin**.

Even if I had A ZILLION PROMISED, I still knew that Findus would be cross to be back at the penguin pool with

Tiffany and all the other penguins.

I bet you all the herrings and kippers and mackerels and sardines and pilchards and goldfish in the sea that he'd much rather have come to my house.

To live on a packet of frozen peas with me!

DAISY'S TROUBLE
INDEX

The trouble with . . .

Going back to bed when you don't want to 234

 Holding eyelids down with your fingers 235

 Letting go of your eyelids when they are too excited 236

 Not being allowed to open just ONE present 237

 Being made to open your birthday cards before you've opened your presents 242

 Birthday wrapping paper 250

Just grabbing
the nearest ones 293

 Llamas 294

 Snorkels 301

 Actual sharks 302

 Trying to fit a whale
in a zoo 303

 Rhinoceroses 304

 Trying to stop a rhino 307

 White rhinos 308

Have you read Daisy's other stories?

DAISY
and the TROUBLE with
KITTENS

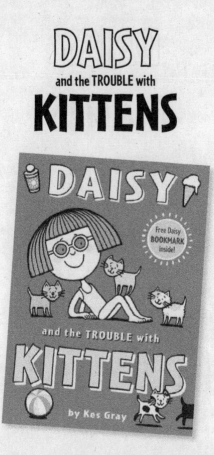

Daisy is going on holiday! In an actual plane to actual Spain!
It's so exciting! She's never seen a palm tree before, or eaten octopus,
or played Zombie Mermaids, or made so many new friends!
TROUBLE is, five of them are small and cute and furry!

DAISY
and the TROUBLE with
CHRISTMAS

It's Christmas and Daisy has been given an actual part in the actual school Christmas play! She has special lines to learn and even a special costume to wear!! Trouble is . . . there's something about baby Jesus that isn't quite special enough . . .

DAISY
and the TROUBLE with
MAGGOTS

Look out, ducks! Look out, canoeists! Daisy is going fishing for the very first time! She's got an actual fishing rod that catches actual fish, an actual bait box full of actual maggots, PLUS an actual fishing catapult that pings, twangs and BLAMS . . . oh dear.